# SINGLE DAD

*A Secret Baby Romance*

## J. P. COMEAU

Copyright © 2020 by J.P. Comeau
All rights reserved.
No part of this book may be reproduced in any form or by any electronic or mechanical means, including information storage and retrieval systems, without written permission from the author, except for the use of brief quotations in a book review.

Single Dad's New Nanny is a work of fiction. All names, characters, places, and occurrences are the product of the author's imagination. Any resemblance to a person, living or deceased, events, or locations is purely coincidental.

## I

**Gavin**

*Wheeze.* "Daddy?" *Wheeze, wheeze.* "Daddy, help!"

I threw the covers off my body and lunged out of bed, only to find my daughter stumbling through my bedroom door. She had her hand against her throat as she struggled to breathe, and I quickly ripped open my bedside table. I cursed under my breath as I jammed my hand into the back, my fingers rummaging around for her fucking inhaler.

And by the time my fingertips found it, I saw tears in her eyes.

"Daddy, please."

I pulled it out of the drawer and shook it. "I got it, princess. It's right here. Stand still for me, okay?"

I cupped the back of her head with only one of my tired eyes open. I felt her struggling as I held the inhaler between her lips, waiting to clock her breathing. I saw tears in her eyes. I saw fear behind her stare. And when I watched her shoulders draw back to inhale another wheezing breath, I sprayed.

And I sprayed.

And I sprayed one more time for good measure.

"Ouch," she whimpered.

I tossed her inhaler onto my bed. "Listen to me. Breathe. In and out. In and out. Slowly, as slowly as you can and as deeply as you can, okay, princess?"

She nodded with tears rushing down her face. "It's not—" *wheeze!*— "working, Daddy."

I spun her around and held her against my chest. "Like me. Feel my breaths and do like me."

I sat on the floor, taking my daughter with me as my hand settled against her chest. I felt my chest rise against her back before she started struggling to mimic my movements. Her tiny hands gripped my pajama pants. Her legs wouldn't stop moving as her body struggled to draw in the air she so desperately needed. And as sweat dripped down the back of my neck, I started the countdown in my head.

*One minute. If she can't breathe in one minute, I need an ambulance.*

"Come on, princess. Be strong for me. You can do this," I whispered.

She shook her head. "I-I-I—" *Wheeze*

I pressed my lips to her ear. "You're the most amazing person I've ever known. Now, I know you can do this. I believe in you. So, relax against me, and let the medicine run its course."

I squeezed my eyes shut and let my lips murmur a prayer to God above who I hoped was watching. I prayed for the medicine to kick in so my daughter wouldn't have to suffer through another hospital visit. She'd already been twice this year, and I wanted to prove to her that we could do this—that *she* could do this.

*Thirty. Thirty-one. Thirty-two.*

"Daddy," she whimpered.

"That's it. That was good. You didn't hiccup my name this time. In through your nose, out through your mouth."

She sniffled. "My nose is stuffy."

"Then, in through your mouth slowly and out even slower. With me, ready?"

*Forty-four. Forty-five. Forty-six.*

I rubbed her chest and felt her melt into me as her breathing finally started to match my own. Relief rushed itself through my veins as her breathing slowly became steady and not so broken. I let a silent tear slip down my cheek. I allowed myself to shed one small tear for the fear I had for my daughter's life.

Then, she collapsed against me while pulling in air.

"Did you have another nightmare?" I asked softly.

She nodded, but she didn't say anything.

"You wanna talk about it?"

She yawned as she shook her head. "Can I sleep with you?"

I scooped her into my arms. "Of course, you can, princess. Come on. I'll tuck you in right beside me."

My fucking ex-wife was the one who had ruined all of this shit for us. She knew she was supposed to keep me up-to-date with the inner workings of her life for the sake of our daughter. But instead, she had hired a nanny who had been so incompetent when it came to our daughter's asthma that she quit and dropped the poor girl on my doorstep while I was still at work.

*My doorstep.*

While no one was home.

And that didn't strike my ex-wife as odd.

"Daddy?"

I tucked her beneath the covers. "Yes, princess?"

*Wheeze.* "It's—it's happen—ing again." *Wheeze!*

I ripped the covers off her body and scooped her into my arms. Fuck the inhaler, she needed a goddamn hospital, and she needed it now. Without a shirt on and only one sock, I snatched up my cell phone, and I raced down the stairs before boogying out my front door. I dug through the glove box of my convertible and found her emergency inhaler and got her to take two deep lungfuls of it, but it didn't alleviate shit. I tossed it to the floorboard and leaped clear over her, landing directly against the leather seats of my new car.

Then, I cranked up the engine and throttled it straight to the emergency room.

"I need help!" I exclaimed as I got out. I scooped my

daughter out without opening the door before rushing into the ER. "Help! My daughter can't breathe!"

Her lips were turning blue as a nurse came and took her out of my arms. Panic ensued around us as the nurse whistled for a doctor and located a gurney. I felt my heart leap into my chest. My sweet, precious little girl couldn't stop crying or catch her breath. It didn't take long for the hospital to admit her, and soon we were whisked away to a private hospital room far away from the prying eyes of the public.

"Mr. Lincoln?"

I spun around and found a woman in a white coat behind me. "Yes, Doctor?"

She handed me a sweater. "I found this in the lost-and-found. I think it's around your size."

I took it from her. "Thank you."

"Mr. Lincoln?"

I whipped back around and found a nurse tending to my daughter. Asia was reaching for me. I excused myself and rushed to her side, taking her hand within my own and kissing her cute little knuckles.

Bulging horror radiated across her face, and it nailed me straight in my gut.

"It's okay. You're safe here, I swear," I whispered.

The nurse was talking at me, but I didn't hear much. I listened to the doctor rattling off what they'd do to my daughter, but I was only half paying attention. I had so many things I needed to fix. I needed to call Jorge and let him know that I wouldn't be there in the morning to start the shooting of the commercial he had hired me to do. I had to get on the phone with my ex-wife and tell her where we were.

I also needed to talk with her about taking the reins with finding a nanny—a competent nanny who could handle the issues that came with our beautiful little girl.

*Who's going to watch her while I'm in Hollywood, meeting with that producer?*

"Daddy?" Her voice sounded clearer, and it pulled me from the depths of my mind.

"Hey there, princess. How're you feeling?"

She nodded softly, her voice hoarse. "Better. Tired."

I stood and kissed her forehead. "Then, why don't you get some rest for me."

"You're not leaving, right?"

I shook my head. "Not after I call Jorge. His jewelry store commercial can wait."

She smiled. "That makes me happy."

I smiled. "*You* make me happy."

And as my daughter fell asleep, gripping my pointer and ring finger together, I wondered what the hell I was going to do.

Who the hell was capable enough to take care of my daughter while I was away? Because it was evident that my ex-wife didn't possess that capability, not even during the designated weeks as per our custody agreement.

## 2

### Eva

"Shit, shit, shit. What am I going to do?"

I paced around my apartment at one in the morning with my hands clasped behind my back. I chewed on the inside of my cheek, wishing that my shift at the restaurant tonight had been nothing but a dream. No, it wasn't possible. I had worked for this restaurant for almost five years. I was slated for a promotion. They couldn't fire me!

And yet, they had.

"Fuck!" I exclaimed.

I kicked the wall and groaned at the pain that shot up the back of my calf. I hopped around before I landed on the couch, prying off my shoe to massage my toes. I sighed as I stared up at the ceiling, my mind turning itself inside out as I tried to figure out what the hell I was going to do.

I had been let go from the only job that kept me afloat, and they didn't even give me a severance package like they usually did.

"Who did I piss off?" I whined.

I sighed as my foot fell to the couch. My arms flopped out, lying against cushions and hovering in midair over the floor as I closed my eyes. I needed to sleep. I wouldn't be able to solve any of my issues tonight. And yet, I had so much nervous energy coursing through my veins that I couldn't sleep no matter how hard I tried.

I couldn't sleep, my foot hurt, and I had no idea what my financial future looked like.

"Great," I murmured.

I mean, sure, waiting tables at that restaurant had only been a part-time gig. But, now I needed something full-time. I needed something to pick up the slack for the job I had just lost, and I needed it to be something other than waiting tables. I'd been a waitress ever since college, and I didn't want that life anymore. I obtained my degree three years ago, so it was time for me to start establishing myself as an adult.

And yet, come next month, I wouldn't even be able to make ends meet.

"Why don't you have a savings account?" I groaned.

*Oh, that's right. You can't find a part-time job. Your degree requires higher education first, which requires more money that you don't have.*

I grabbed a pillow and put it over my face before I started screaming into it. I screamed, and I screamed until I lost my voice, then I screamed some more for good measure. I'd never felt this helpless in all my life. I'd never felt so lost and so alone, despite the connections I had made for myself mostly, at the spa where I worked part-time, too.

*At least I still have them.*

I drew in a deep breath and let the pillow flop onto the floor. I turned onto my side toward the television. I grabbed the remote, turning on the first slab of trashy television I could find. Trashy reality TV was the secret love of my life. I loved watching it, if only because it always served as a reminder that no matter how bad my life got, it would never be quite *that* bad.

And before I knew it, my cell phone alarm went off in my bedroom and jolted me upright.

"Ugh, I would've been better off not sleeping," I hissed.

I pushed my tired ass off the couch and limped on my bruised foot into the kitchen. I pulled the pot of coffee out of my fridge and poured a tall glass before chugging it back. Dousing myself in coffee always worked wonders, but today I was more sluggish than usual.

But, I knew going in for my morning shift at the spa would take my mind off things.

I sloshed around and got ready, trying to make do with what I had. My hair went up into a messy bun, and I counteracted the shaggy look with a nice pair of earrings and some muted makeup. I put on a lovely, sleek outfit that was fitting for a daytime manager, even if the part-time position didn't even provide me with enough to pay my bills, much less pay my student loans off.

"Jesus Christ, help me," I whispered.

I picked up the bill from the table next to the front door, and it made my stomach turn. That monthly amount was almost ungodly, and I wanted to tear it to shreds. It made me so angry that education in this country cost so damn much and that a degree still didn't get me anywhere.

"Nothing but a money pit, if you ask me," I murmured.

I stopped on my way to work and picked up a large iced coffee with two shots of espresso and sweet cream galore. I sucked it down to the halfway point before I even walked through the back entrance. By the time I got to my office, I had tossed the empty plastic container into the trash can.

I wasn't alone for long, though. Because the second my ass hit my office chair, I heard Ginger's voice pipe up behind me.

"Please tell me you heard about the weekend getaway Yuslan took Guadalupe on this past weekend."

I sighed. "No, Ginger. I didn't hear."

She stepped into my office and closed the door. "Well, I heard that he whisked her away to this cute little indoor water world hotel thing. Did you know Guadalupe loves to swim? Yeah, I heard that he took her to one of those places and bought them weekend passes so they could go do whatever they wanted on the resort grounds."

I nodded mindlessly. "Sounds nice."

"Oh! Get this. I also saw Margo with her handsome boo-thang at Renoir's, of all places. You know, that French bistro across town? I think something big's going down with them. You don't ever go to a place like Renoir's without something big going down."

I pinched the bridge of my nose. "Ginger, I just need some time t—"

"Oh, oh, oh! I'm not even done just yet. I'm saving the best for last. My friend Gavin? You know, Gavin Lincoln? The handsome A-list Hollywood actor? Yeah, he was in the hospital with his daughter last night because she's got asthma. And I heard from Jorge that he couldn't make it to his commercial shoot this morning."

I slowly spun around. "*The* Gavin Lincoln?"

She nodded slowly. "Uh, huh! The one and only."

"Is his daughter all right?"

"I mean, I think so? I wish there were a way I could help, though. Poor guy needs some serious help, and he's got a selfish, lazy-ass ex-wife who doesn't give a shit about anyone other than herself. I swear, he and that cute little girl of his deserve better. You know Jorge told me she didn't even show up to the hospital last night?"

I blinked. "Wait. Did you say he needed help?"

She shrugged. "I mean, yeah. All Hollywood actors nowadays have nannies and such."

I crossed my leg over my knee. "How bad is his daughter's asthma? You think that's why they can't find good help or something?"

She blinked. "It's bad, and that's not even gossip. Everyone who's anyone who's a fan of that man knows that his daughter's asthma is damn-near debilitating," she said as she lowered her voice to a whisper. "And Jorge tells me it's only getting worse."

"Poor guy."

"Right? Poor guy, indeed."

Ginger stood in my office, obviously waiting for me to respond. But, I was too deep in thought. I mean, *the* Gavin Lincoln? Needing a nanny? Was I crazy to even consider it? The man was drop-dead gorgeous. The epitome of strong and sexy. And dammit, the dad thing looked absolutely incredible on him. Not that I was some super-fan. But, he had been taking over Hollywood recently, and I'd seen nothing short of four separate movies in the past year where he took the leading role and completely ran away with it.

But, the idea of nannying for someone like him intimidated me beyond words.

Ginger's voice hit my ears again. "You know, I should give Gavin a call. I know he hasn't been out and about lately. Maybe he needs to get out and socialize for a little bit."

I blinked. "You know him well enough that you can just call him?"

She shrugged. "I mean, Jorge does. They're best friends. Didn't you know that?"

I shook my head as Guadalupe peeked around the corner. "We talking about her *alto, oscuro, y guapo* man?"

Ginger wiggled her eyebrows. "We're talking about an *alto, oscuro, y guapo*. But, according to what I last heard, the man hasn't even dated since he and his ex-wife split, the bitch. You know she hired a nanny that had absolutely no idea how to deal with her daughter's asthma, and the woman quit by dumping the poor kid on Gavin's porch while he was at work. At work!"

My eyes widened. "Wait, are you serious? How long did she have to wait there for someone to come get her?"

Ginger shrugged. "How should I know? I'm just the messenger."

My heart went out to that little girl. I could only imagine how traumatizing that must've been for her. It made my blood boil, to be honest. I'd had my fair share of trauma like that from the broken family I came from, and it made me sick to know of another innocent young girl going through much of the same shit I endured as a child.

"You thinking pretty hard over there?" Guadalupe asked.

I shrugged. "Just turning something around, that's all."

Ginger giggled. "Thinking about lining up a run-in with Gavin? Because I can totally help you with that."

I turned my chair back toward my computer. "I think that I need to get started on work."

Guadalupe and Ginger kept talking as they closed my office door, but I couldn't concentrate. I didn't care what Gavin looked like or who he was. My heart only went out to his daughter. It not only sounded like he needed help, but it also sounded like she needed stability. Someone she could genuinely rely on while her parents were out chasing their dreams. Not that I faulted them for that, but a child needed a foundation. A child needed someone to root them to the earth, so to speak.

After all, I needed a job, and it sounded like that sweet little girl needed a security blanket.

So, after I clocked in, I found myself searching around on the internet for pictures of Gavin with his daughter, trying to get an idea of what their relationship was like, at least in the public eye.

## 3

### Gavin

"When can we go home, Daddy?"

I smoothed my daughter's hair out of her face. "Soon, princess. I promise, okay?"

She sniffled. "No more nights here, okay?"

I kissed her forehead. "Let's see what the doctor sa—"

"Gavin!" The piercing, tinny sound of my ex-wife's voice barreled down the hallway.

"Asia! Gavin! Where are you guys?"

My daughter sighed. "So loud."

I patted her arm. "Hold on, you get some rest, okay?"

"Asia!" she shrieked.

I bolted for the door and ripped it open. "Can you keep it down, Marissa?"

She glared at me. "Where's my daughter? I want to see her."

I ushered her inside. "About time you showed up."

She hissed at me. "Not much I can do about an asthma attack in the middle of a photo shoot."

"A photo shoot? At two in the morning? You really expect me to believe—"

Then, Marissa put on her best "concerned Mom" voice. "Oh, my poor, sweet girl. How are you feeling? Have you had anything to drink? I brought your favorite."

I closed the door and watched as she pulled out one of the few drinks Asia couldn't stand. And it made me shake my head.

"Here," Marissa said as she opened the fruit punch pouch. "I grabbed it at a gas station just for you."

Asia shook her head. "No, thank you."

Marissa paused. "No, thank you? I mean, your manners are wonderful, but since when don't you want a fruit punch pouch?"

"Since forever," I murmured.

Asia giggled, and Marissa shot me a look over her shoulder. How the fuck a mother couldn't remember one of the things her own child hated was beyond me. Nevertheless, my ex-wife decided to drop it, and I was glad she did. Because usually, she made drama out of the slightest things that inconvenienced her.

"Why don't you tell Mommy all about what happened, yeah?" Marissa asked.

She turned back to Asia and waited patiently, but I saw my daughter staring over her mother's shoulder at me.

"It's okay. Go ahead," I said.

Marissa shot me a look as she craned her neck back. "No one in this room needs your permission for my daughter to talk to me."

"Mom, stop," Asia whispered.

She turned her attention back to our daughter. "Come on. It's okay. You know you can talk to me about anything, right?"

I rolled my eyes at that sentiment. Yeah, anyone could talk to Marissa about anything. If they were ready for an hour lecture on everything, they were doing wrong.

*Why did I marry this woman again?*

Oh. Right. Because getting her pregnant while not wedded didn't sit well with her conservative Romanian parents.

As their stunted conversation ensued, I made my way into the corner and sat down. Up until recently, Asia's asthma had been easy to control. If she felt an attack coming on, one or two pumps from her inhaler kicked it to the curb. But, lately? Her attacks were more frequent.

Which had me worried.

The kicker, though, was the fact that they started getting worse when Marissa left town for this new modeling job. And she wasn't going to be done with the damn job for at least three weeks. While she was still in the state of Florida, she was up there by the Georgia line snapping pictures for some winter magazine spread she was being featured in, which meant that taking care of Asia fell onto my shoulders until she got back.

And while we had an okay co-parenting relationship, there was a trend with Marissa's job. The time she spent away from home—and away from Asia—kept getting longer and longer.

*I have to find stability for Asia's life.*

I knew that was what caused these attacks, and I knew they wouldn't stop until Asia got what she needed. Bouncing between my house and my ex-wife's place whenever she had to go off and do something simply wasn't cutting it. And with all my might, I wished I could rewind time and take Marissa to court in order to get an on-paper custody agreement.

The two of us had agreed to talk shit out like adults when it came to Asia's schedule.

But, I didn't realize it would lead to such disjointed time between the two of us.

Marissa's cooing pulled me from the recesses of my mind. "Yeah, it's okay, sweetheart. You just get some rest. Mommy will be right here when you wake up, okay?"

Asia sniffled. "Daddy, too?"

I walked up and sat on the edge of the bed. "I'll always be here, princess. Okay?"

I took her small hand within mine and watched my daughter's watery eyes find my gaze. It broke my heart to see her so tired and so confused. But, she was the safest in this hospital. And even if we had to stay another night, it would be worth it, even if it did spark a fight between Marissa and me.

"Can I speak with you for a second, please?" she asked.

I sighed. "Can it wait? I'm really not in the mood to fight."

She scoffed, "I don't want to fight with you. I just want to talk about our schedules." Which was code for "this job is going to take longer than I thought."

"Sure. Yeah. Let's step outside," I said.

Asia gripped my hand. "Come back soon?"

I leaned forward and kissed her forehead. "I promise."

Marissa kissed our daughter's hand. "Me, too. Okay?"

Asia didn't acknowledge her, and that told me everything I needed to know. As much as I respected Marissa for trying—and as much as I loved her for giving me Asia—she wasn't cut out to be the stability Asia needed. She wasn't willing to compromise her career like I'd had to do so many times in order to pick up the slack she had dropped. She wasn't willing to do what was necessary to change her life to give Asia what she needed.

I knew Asia would do better being with me the majority of the time.

The issue was convincing Marissa of that.

The two of us stood and made our way outside. My ex-wife grabbed the doorknob and closed the door until only a sliver of a crack was all that remained of the light inside Asia's hospital room.

Then, she looked up at me with a determined gaze. "My job in Georgia's going to keep me gone for another couple of weeks."

I nodded. "I figured as much."

"Hey, don't take that tone of voice with me."

I shrugged. "What tone?"

She put her hand on her hip. "You know the tone I'm talking about. The one that says, 'of course you'd keep working. Why not? It's all about you anyway.'"

"At least you understand, then."

"And what am I supposed to do, Gavin? Huh? I can't just back out of the contract. I already signed it, and in my contract, it stipulated that the job would take three weeks but possibly five."

I blinked. "You didn't tell me the 'possibly five' part."

She crossed her arms over her chest. "I take it you've got some job or whatever coming up?"

"Does it matter? Look, we both know what's going to happen. You're going to win, you're going to be gone for another two weeks, and then you'll pick up Asia and drop her at my doorstep whenever you need to be gone for another month."

"What's wrong with that?"

I took a step toward her. "What's wrong is you're doing it when your schedule allows it. You're not doing it based on what Asia needs. She needs a schedule. A routine. Something she can rely on."

She glared up at me. "Which is why she's got her mother."

"Oh, is that what you call the half-assed job you put in of hiring a nanny who wasn't even trained in how to take care of someone with asthma? Asia was standing on my doorstep for almost a fucking hour before I—"

She pointed her finger in my face. "Don't you dare cuss at

me, Gavin Lincoln. I'm not your wife anymore. I don't need to take that shit from you."

"Then do what you know is right for our child. Sit down with me, let's come up with a schedule of rotating weekends where we get her, and she can be with me during the school year breaks."

She leaned back. "Oh, so you can go off and work all through the school year, and I'm stuck at home doing the stay-at-home Mom thing?"

"If you didn't want to be a parent and put your child's needs first, then we shouldn't have had a child."

She scoffed as her voice raised. "Do you even know the definition of 'accident?'"

The second I heard the sound of little feet scurrying away from the door, my face fell. Marissa gasped as I slammed the door open just in time to see Asia wiggle her way beneath the covers. I heard her soft cries, and it broke my heart. But, Marissa shoved me out of the way to rush toward her bed.

"Come here, sweetheart. Mommy didn't mean what—"

Asia pulled away. "Don't touch me. I don't want you."

Marissa jerked away like she'd been shot. "What?"

Then, Asia peeked out from beneath the covers and held her hand out to me. "Daddy, please?"

I walked over to her, sat down, and took her hand. "I'm right here, princess."

I felt my ex-wife glaring at the profile of my face. "Thanks for nothing. I'm going to go get a legitimate doctor instead of talking to these thick-headed nurses."

And when she stormed out of the room, Asia tugged me onto the bed.

I climbed in beside her and cradled her close, my heart breaking with every tear that fell from her eyes. I stroked my fingers through her hair and shushed her softly against her ear, hoping and praying she'd fall asleep before Marissa dared to enter this room again. The woman was a walking train wreck. Nothing but a nice few fucks and some good pictures together to help my career before she got pregnant and demanded we get married to save her own skin. I tolerated three years with that woman, trying to make things work for the sake of Asia.

And now, I was trying desperately to piece together her broken life with a woman who didn't give a fuck about anything but herself.

"I love you so much," I whispered.

Asia tucked herself closely against me, and soon her breaths evened out. I held her until she fell asleep, then eased myself out of bed to call Jorge again. I needed to keep him abreast of what was going on, and the fact that a doctor hadn't come by to discharge us today meant we were probably staying another night. And now, with Marissa's change of plans, there was no way in hell I'd be free to shoot that commercial anytime soon—unless Asia could come to the set with me.

"Hey, hey, hey. How's the little one doing?" Jorge asked as he picked up my call.

I sighed as I stood in the corner. "We still haven't been discharged."

"You know, I figured that might happen. Asia's attacks have been pretty rough lately. They probably wanna keep her to see if she has another one so they can find an origin point or something."

I chuckled. "I keep forgetting your mother had asthma."

"Yep. Did this many times with her, too. Don't worry; it's just protocol. And I've pushed back the commercial shoot to the weekend so Asia can get home and rest before you leave."

I sighed. "Actually, about that."

"Oh, boy."

"Marissa finally showed up."

He paused. "Better late than never?"

I shook my head. "That excuse only works so many times."

"You right, you right. So, when will you be free?"

"That depends. If I can bring Asia to set with me? I can shoot as soon as she's feeling better."

"I mean, not that I don't love your daughter, but kids on sets usually don't work out as planned."

I shrugged. "Then, at least another two weeks."

He hissed. "Son of a bitch."

"Ex-husband of a bitch, is more like it," I murmured.

Jorge barked with laughter. "Oh, dude, I don't know what the hell you were thinking."

"Just trying to do right by the family I created, even if it wasn't planned."

"Which is why it kills me that you have to pay for sex. Any woman out there would be willing to thrust themselves at your feet, yet you pay out the ass for escorts. Why do you do this shit to yourself?"

I shrugged. "Anonymity? Those women sign NDA's for days before I even get in their presence. Can't really do that to a regular, ordinary girl."

"Well, maybe you should start thinking about getting someone in your life who's a bit regular and ordinary."

"Ugh, that sounds like a dream. But, for now, I'd just settle for some damn help."

He snickered. "Well, I can't come help, but Ginger might have found a couple of people interested in helping you out."

I blinked. "What do you mean?"

"You remember Eva? You met her briefly."

"Uh... you'll have to be more specific than that."

"Brown hair? Tanned skin? Kind of slim, but legs for days?"

I clicked my tongue. "Yeah, no. Nothing's coming to mind."

He sighed. "Green eyes? I mean, emerald green. That bright kind of green you can see coming from a mile away."

Then, it clicked. "Oh! Yes, yes, yes, yes. I remember her now. Works at the spa and a restaurant or something, right?"

"Well, she doesn't work at the restaurant anymore. She's looking for another part-time job and—"

"Yeah, I don't need part-time help."

"Will you just listen instead of cutting me off, dude? Look, she's got great qualifications. And I bet if you make the pay worth her while you could buy her full-time status. Just think about it, okay? She's got evenings free and her weekends, and she could at least be a jumping point for helping you a little bit now until you find someone who can help you the way you need."

I licked my lips. "Yeah, yeah. I'll think about it."

"Great. Now, you keep me updated on Asia. And we'll talk once you guys get discharged. I'll come over with cake. It'll be a blast."

I smiled. "Sounds good. We'll talk soon."

"Talk soon, man."

And as I turned back around to look at my daughter sleeping helplessly in a hospital bed much too big for her, I turned the idea over in my head.

*Part-time help is better than no-time help.*

So, I shot Jorge an email and asked him to get me Eva's resume.

Couldn't hurt to at least take a look at it.

## 4

### Eva

"Psst."

I unlocked my office for another morning of work before I heard the sound again.

"Psssst. Eva."

I paused. "Guadalupe?"

She eased around the corner. "Hey, we need to talk in your office."

I blinked. "Okay...? Everything all right?"

She simply stared at the door, waiting for me to open it. So, I quickly unlocked it and ushered her inside while panic gripped my throat. Had I done something wrong? Was I about to get fired? That would be just my luck, pissing off Guadalupe and Yuslan so much that they fired me from the first officially titled job I had ever held in my life. I walked into my office behind her and quickly closed the door. If I were about to get fired, I didn't want anyone to hear my crying because I'd drown this office in my sorrows.

"So, my niece is looking for daytime work to take on, and the arrangement would be perfect."

I turned to face her. "Sorry. Uh, what arrangement?"

She paused. "Ginger hasn't told you?"

I cocked my head. "Told me what?"

She lowered her voice to a whisper. "Gavin Lincoln personally requested your resume along with my niece's. He's looking to put together nannying help for his daughter!" She was so excited that she squeaked the last word, which made me giggle. Then, it hit me.

"Wait, he asked for mine, too?" I asked.

Guadalupe nodded. "Oh, yes, he did. And I figured the arrangement between you and my niece would be perfect. She's looking for some daytime work, and you're looking for evening work. Correct?"

I nodded. "Right, yeah."

"Then, it's settled! My daughter is a trained CNA, so if you don't have any certifications or training in how to deal with those who are asthmatic—"

I smiled as I interrupted her. "Actually, I do."

She placed her hands on my shoulders. "This is going to be a good thing. I just know it."

"I really hope you're right, Guadalupe."

Ginger came bursting into the office. "Did she say yes? Please tell me I can call Jorge now."

Guadalupe gave her a thumbs up. "Call away!"

I narrowed my eyes. "This was a set-up?"

Guadalupe patted my cheek. "A set-up for your future, sweetheart. Just take it and be thankful."

Ginger squealed and rushed down the hallway, yelling at someone to fetch her phone for her. Guadalupe raised up onto her tiptoes and gave me a kiss on my forehead, and for a split second, it seemed like everything was going to be just fine. Guadalupe had a way of pulling things out of her ass that benefitted all of us when we needed it most, and I hoped it was my time for that.

Because my first student loan installment was three weeks away, and I didn't have the cash flow to pay for it.

"Oh, and by the way," Guadalupe said as she started out of my office, "Mr. Lincoln's already hired my niece for his daytime shift. We just wanted to make sure you were on board before we got your interview with him scheduled."

I shook my head. "Three peas in a pod, you all are."

Ginger poked her head above Guadalupe's in the doorway. "How does dinner tonight sound? Seven? At Radcliffe's?"

I shook my head and shrugged. "Sure?"

Ginger went back to talking on the phone. "She agreed. Yes, let's get this set-up. You call Gavin and—"

Guadalupe shut my office door, closing off the rest of the conversation. And by the time I was done with my workday at the spa, Ginger had a time and place set up for Gavin and me to meet. My hands trembled as I made my way home. I spent over an hour trying to pick out the right outfit. I mean, it wasn't a date, so it didn't have to be sexy. But, I was about to meet up with an A-list Hollywood actor in one of the finest, most discreet restaurants in the city for a job interview.

"What the hell do I wear to something like this?" I whispered.

After finally settling on some high-waisted black pants, black heels, and a white ruffled blouse, I opted for some sparkling jewelry since the colors were pretty tame. I painted on some red lipstick before wiping it off, then chose a nice, cool shade. The rich purple made my eyes pop, but it didn't make me look like I was hoping to get lucky by the end of this dinner.

And once the clock ticked over to six-thirty, I was out the door.

"Radcliffe's. Radcliffe's. Come on, where's the sign?"

My GPS got me to the road it sat on, but I drove up and down it, trying to find the damned sign. At first, I thought I was going crazy. Then, I thought maybe I had punched in the address wrong. But, after driving back down the road a fifth time, I saw it.

Tucked down at the beginning of an alleyway, of all places.

"Oh, boy," I murmured.

The only reason why I felt comfortable parking my car and getting out was that everyone knew of this place. If they hadn't been there, they at least knew where it was and the kinds of food they served. It was easily the most upscale place downtown, and I felt sorely underdressed, just stepping into the restaurant.

But, the maître d' must have noticed me because the second I walked inside, he appeared at my side. "This way, Miss Johnson." His accent was thick, and I couldn't place it.

"I'm sorry, do we know each other?"

He smiled kindly. "Mr. Lincoln is waiting for you upstairs. I have been told to escort you once you arrived."

I nodded slowly. "Well, then, by all means, lead the way. And thank you."

He bowed softly. "You're quite welcome. It is an honor."

As we made our way for the stairs, I couldn't stop rubbernecking around. Everyone was dressed to the nines and decked out in their finest jewelry and fabrics. There was soft music playing from a live band in the corner that looked like they had come pre-programmed with the entire restaurant. The hand-carved crown moldings that adorned the upper portion of the walls were breathtaking. The fact that all of the tables and booths had these black marble tops with sparkling brown specks in them made me gawk every time we passed by one. Even as we ascended the steps, the mahogany banister ushered us all the way up to the top.

And when the maître d' opened a door at the top of the steps, I found myself walking into a room that had only one table placed in the middle with a crackling fireplace off to the side—and a very handsome Hollywood man standing to his feet.

"Eva Johnson. It's good to meet you again," Gavin said.

I swallowed hard to pull myself out of my trance, and I moved just quickly enough to shake his hand without him having to stand there, waiting for me. "Likewise, Mr. Lincoln."

He held his hand out toward the table. "Please, call me Gavin. Have a seat. There's wine already poured, and I took the liberty of ordering us some soup for an appetizer. It's their house recipe, and it's outstanding. Everyone has to try it at least once."

I smiled as I walked to my seat. "Sounds delightful, thank you."

"Daddy, Daddy, Daddy! Look at what I found!"

I heard Gavin chuckle as I pivoted to find the source of the voice. "What is it, princess?"

"I found a pencil that Mr. Black had."

I furrowed my brow. "Mr. Black?"

Gavin crouched down to the level of who I assumed was his daughter. "She means the maître d', Giuseppe."

*Italian, of course.*

"Would you like some paper to draw on? I keep a notebook in my purse."

The shy little girl buried herself in her father's arms, then peeked her eyes out over his muscles. "Please?"

I smiled. "Of course. Here, I'll set it on your father's chair."

I dug around in my purse and made sure there wasn't anything written in the notebook that couldn't be ruined. And after pulling out a few pages worth of notes I had taken, I walked the notebook over and sat it on Gavin's seat. I backed up and took my place at the table, watching as the hesitant girl pulled her father along while she crept toward the chair. Then, she swiped it up and burrowed beneath the table.

"She likes it under there, with the tablecloth and everything. Makes her feel like she's in a fort," Gavin said.

I nodded. "I used to do that all the time with my sheets as a little girl. My parents actually bought a second kitchen table so they'd have a place to eat and I'd have a place to play."

The girl giggled underneath the table. "I'm gonna do this at home."

Gavin sat down across the table from me. "So, I took a look at your resume, and it's pretty impressive."

I nodded. "I'm glad you think so."

"It looks like you held a couple of nannying gigs while in college?"

"I did, yes. They were part-time, and then overnights on the weekends. I did a lot of babysitting when I was in high school as well. The references are at the bottom if you'd like to give anyone a call."

He slid his napkin into his lap. "Oh, don't worry. I already did. It's why I felt comfortable scheduling this meeting."

*Keep it together, Eva.* "Yes, yes. Of course, you would. This is a huge decision."

His eyes met mine. "The biggest. I don't entrust just anyone with my daughter."

"And if I had children, it would be the exact same way."

"Do you want children someday?"

An odd question for an interview, but it felt more like a conversation anyway, so I obliged. "One day, yes. Maybe two or three. I know one day I'll be a mother, but the number itself doesn't hold a lot of weight. I guess I'll just have children until I feel like I can't handle anymore."

He smiled, and it lit up the entire room. "So, tell me about yourself. Other than the monetary necessities everyone else has on this planet, why do you want to go back to nannying?

## 5

## Gavin

I watched Eva contemplate my question, and watching her gave me a chance to really study her. Dammit, she was more beautiful than I even remembered—and those eyes. They looked more piercing with that lipstick on her full, lovely lips.

"To be honest? I hadn't really considered it," she said.

I blinked. "Really? Why's that?"

She shrugged. "Well, as you can tell by the dates on my resume, I was recently fired from a job I had at a restaurant where I worked for years. And I'm in dire need of filling that financial void before some payments come due. A lot of the nannying and babysitting I did wasn't for the money but just to help people out. They needed someone to watch their kids, and I was more than willing to give of my time."

"That's very virtuous of you."

She reached for her wine glass. "Oh, I loved it. Children and I get along spectacularly. But, the girls at the spa caught wind of my losing my job, and then you hired Guadalupe's niece to work for you during the day. I figured this could be a way I could help someone out in need and fill the financial void in the process."

I reached for my wine glass as well. "I appreciate your honesty. And forgive how formal this all feels. Asia wanted to get dressed up and go out tonight, and who can say no to something like that?"

She giggled. "I think it's really sweet."

My heart warmed at her words. "Thank you, genuinely. And you're right, I have hired Guadalupe's niece for the day shift to help me out. But, I still need someone for a night shift. Possible overnights, too."

I saw her turning over my words behind her eyes, and I knew she was hung up over the "overnight" issue. The truth of the matter was that sometimes I didn't get home from a set until one or two in the morning. I couldn't just leave my daughter at the house by herself to sleep. Someone needed to be there.

I sipped my wine. "This will be a lot easier if you simply spit out what you're thinking."

Eva sipped her own wine before she drew in a deep breath. "Well, Monday through Friday, I work at the spa.

Every weekday, from six in the morning until two in the afternoon. And while I'm not sure where you live, I know that with this constant traffic, anywhere outside of a ten-block radius is going to take me at least forty minutes to get through with my car, versus just walking from my place."

I leaned back in my seat. "And going home in the middle of the night would detract from the sleep you can get for your other job."

"Exactly."

I puffed out my cheeks with a sigh. "Well, I've got guest bedrooms and a guesthouse that you're more than welcome to stay in. My home would be your home. Most of the bedrooms have attached bathrooms, so your privacy wouldn't be an issue. And if you're too tired to drive yourself to work, I don't see why you can't borrow Lucas to take you to work."

She blinked. "Lucas?"

I nodded. "My driver. I know that doesn't fix the whole 'lack of sleep' issue, but there are a ton of great coffee places he could take you to before getting you to the spa for your shift."

I knew it was only a temporary solution, but I grew excited when she smiled. She sipped her wine, and I had to resist the urge to watch her lips as they wrapped around the edge of the crystal glass. What was that color? Black? Dark red? Navy?

Eva cleared her throat. "I could make that work, definitely."

I chuckled. "Sounds like we have a promising future, then."

I felt a tug on my pant leg before Asia's voice sounded. "Is our food here yet?"

Our waiter's voice rang out into the room. "Got your soup right here, actually."

Asia climbed up into her chair. "Yay!"

Eva sniffed the air. "That smells amazing. What kind of soup is it?"

The waiter set our bowls in front of us. "A ginger and tomato bisque with parsnips. Our house special."

Asia picked up her spoon. "Is there bread, too?"

The waiter put the basket of bread right in front of her. "As much of it as you want."

"Yay!"

Eva reached for a piece of bread. "I'm with her. Soup with bread is the perfect start to any meal."

For a little while, the table fell silent as we all dipped our bread into the soup and ate our fill. Asia abandoned her spoon in order to tip the bowl up to her lips. I shook my head as she started gulping it down.

"Asia, you know your table manners," I said.

Then, Eva's beautiful voice sounded. "Actually, in some cultures, they tip their bowls up just like that to drink their soup."

Ava put her bowl down long enough to stick out her tongue, and I tickled her side.

"Better watch where you point that thing because my fingers are quicker than your legs," I said.

Eva giggled. "Here, I'll join you, Asia. If that's all right?"

My daughter peeked over at her, and I watched as Eva scooped her bowl into her hands. She held it up, refusing to drink even one drop until she got the okay from my daughter. I watched the two of them like a hawk as my little girl studied her. And the truth of the matter was that if Eva couldn't bond with my daughter, no amount of schedule finagling would benefit us.

But then, my daughter nodded and went back to slurping her soup, followed by Eva with her own slurping sounds.

"Hell, why not?" I asked.

Asia giggled. "You said a yucky word."

I took my bowl in my hands. "And don't you forget that it's yucky, either."

Eva nodded. "Yep. Some words make people happy, and some words make people sad. And we shouldn't make people sad with our words."

Asia shook her head. "Nope. Only happy faces."

Eva smiled. "Exactly. Only happy faces for us."

The exchange warmed my heart as the three of us resumed the slurping of our soups. I felt relieved, more than anything, that this was going so well. So, I decided to sit back for a little while and watch the two girls interact. At first, there was silence after we ordered entrees. I settled on the surf and turf while my daughter ordered a big bowl of noodles, and Eva, ironically enough, ordered the same thing I did.

I wasn't sure if she could put away that kind of food, but it was nice to be in the presence of a woman who ate something other than a bare salad.

"Whatcha drawing there?" Eva asked.

Asia hid the notebook from her. "It's a secret. Can't see until it's done."

Eva gasped playfully. "Am I gonna love it?"

Asia nodded. "I hope so."

"Will we get to color it together afterward?"

Asia's eyes lit up. "You like to color?"

Eva giggled. "I love to color. I use markers because they're my favorite. What's your favorite?"

Asia loosened her grip on the notepad. "Well, I kind of like paint. But, if we have to use pencil-like things, I really like colored pencils. Or gel pens!"

Eva started digging around in her purse. "A girl after my own heart. Here, I have a stack of gel pens at the bottom of my purse."

Asia squealed. "You do? Do you have pink? *Please* say you have pink."

Eva barked with laughter. "I've got various shades of pink in here. It's my favorite color. I'll pull them out and—"

*Crash!*

Something broke in the kitchen, and the sound ricocheted off the corners of the room we all sat in. Asia jumped so high out of her chair that I thought she'd fall onto the floor, so I reached out to steady her. But, when I heard that tell-tale wheezing, my heart stopped in my chest.

"Dadd-ddy," she wheezed.

I stood up. "I've got your inhaler in my pocket. I just have to…"

I started feeling around for her inhaler, but I couldn't locate it. I jammed my hand into my inside suit pockets and turned my hip pockets inside out. I looked around, wondering if it had fallen onto the floor when I had sat down.

But then, Eva's soothing voice caught my ears. "Come here. Let me help, Asia. We're going to do something fun, okay?"

Asia started panting. "I need—I can't—"

Eva took her hands. "Yes, you can. You got spooked, and your body locked up. You don't need your inhaler, I promise. You just need to relax."

I watched with pointed eyes as Asia began to cry.

"Please. Daddy—I just—"

Eva cupped her cheek. "Trust me, okay? Can you do that? Just this once?"

And when Asia nodded, I slowly sat back down.

"All right, think of your favorite place in the whole world, Asia. Mine is the ocean. I love the feeling of the sand between my toes and water sloshing over my skin. What's yours?"

My daughter continued wheezing, and I started growing worried. But nonetheless, she answered the question.

"Chuck—Chuck E. Cheese."

Eva sat down and carried my daughter with her. "Oh,

that's a great place. Pizza's my favorite food. What kind of toppings do you like?"

My daughter clung to Eva. "Cheese—and…and pineapple."

"Oh, that sounds yummy. I'm a ham, bacon, and mushroom person myself. And, I like dipping it in ranch."

Asia attempted to laugh. "That's gross."

Eva shrugged. "Eh, not for everyone. But it's my favorite. What's your favorite game to play at Chuck E. Cheese? I like the ones that flash and give you lots of tickets."

And to my surprise, Asia's wheezing finally started dying down. "The, uh—the—uh… the pinball? No, the uh, skyball?"

"Skeeball?"

Asia smiled. "That's the one."

"Oh, I'm terrible at skeeball. The last time I tried it, I threw the ball so hard that it came flying right back at me! Hit me in the shins and everything."

When I heard Asia draw in a near-lungful of air to laugh, I relaxed fully against my chair. I didn't know how the hell Eva had managed to do it, but she had calmed my daughter down and thwarted the attack without her inhaler. I felt something pressing against my ankle, and I looked down, only to groan when I saw Asia's inhaler beneath my fucking seat.

I plucked it off the floor and slid it into the breast pocket of my suit as Eva scooped up my daughter.

"Here, let's get you some water. See how that goes down, okay?" she asked.

Asia gripped Eva's pant leg. "Will you stay here?"

Eva crouched down beside her. "Of course. I'll be right here."

I watched my daughter gulp down some ice water, and not once did she cough. She didn't wheeze or begin to panic, or hiccup or cough. The attack was completely gone, and I was shellshocked.

"Are you a CNA as well?" I asked.

Eva peeked over at me. "I'm not, no. But, my brother had asthma growing up. So, I kind of know what it looks like. I helped him out a lot when we were growing up, so it's just kind of natural, I guess."

I didn't hesitate with the offer because I knew I'd never find anyone else who bonded with my daughter tonight like she just had.

"Six nights a week with Sundays off. I'd pay you a grand a week. And during the week, if the nights are late, you can pick out your own guest bedroom and bathroom to store your stuff and occupy. Plus, use of my driver, Lucas, to get you to work if you're too tired to drive."

She nodded. "I accept your offer, Mr. Lincoln."

I grabbed my wine glass. "A toast, then, to your new job."

She stood with my daughter holding onto her pant leg still and reached for her goblet. "To my new job and a new adventure."

And as we clinked our glasses together, I hoped I was making the right choice with Eva. I saw the way she stared at me, the way her eyes lingered a bit longer than usual. I saw her lean body beneath her clothes and thought about what it might feel like to have every inch of her long, luscious legs wrapped around me. I hoped she wasn't the wrong decision, though, and not just for my daughter's sake but for my sake, as well.

Because a woman with a kind smile and a great set of legs always made me come undone.

## 6

**Eva**

"Yes! Yes! Yes! Yes!"

I held my pillow to my face and squealed into it as I kicked my legs. I felt my shoes go flying off before they hit the wall, and it only punctuated my sincere excitement. I couldn't believe it. I had just scored the nannying job of a lifetime! Four grand a month? I had never gotten paid that much at the peak of my waitressing career.

"Oh, my God. I did it," I whispered.

I fell back onto my bed and reached for my cell phone. I needed to call Ginger and Margo. I knew they were waiting for my call, and I couldn't contain my happiness any longer. I propped my pillow beneath my head and dialed Ginger's number. I merged the call with Margo's line ringing on the other end.

And when the two of them picked up, I yelped. "I did it!"

Ginger gasped. "No. You got the job?"

Margo sighed. "Sorry, my ear's ringing. What was that?"

I clicked my tongue. "I got the job, Margo. You know, that nannying gig with *the* Gavin Lincoln?"

Margo paused. "Holy shit, he offered it to you on the spot?"

I giggled profusely. "Right? Yeah, he did. Four grand a month to help out Monday through Saturday. Sundays off. I'm going to be able to pay my student loans, you guys. And on time. Hell, with that kind of money, I could probably snowball it and get it paid off in half the time!"

Ginger hissed. "Yes! This is perfect. This is exactly what you needed right now."

Margo giggled. "I'm happy for you. Really."

I sighed with relief. "I appreciate it."

The sound of Ginger flopping down onto her beanbag came through on the other end of the line. "Oh, no, no, no, no. You're going to tell us all about this interview. Rumor has it the two of you went out to *dinner*."

Margo snickered. "A job interview over dinner? Where did you go?"

I stared up at my ceiling. "Well, Asia wanted to get dressed up and go out, so that's why the dinner happened."

"Yet, you still haven't answered Margo's question. Where did you guys eat?"

I paused for a while before I finally answered. "Radcliffe's."

The two girls gasped practically on cue, and I rolled my eyes. I knew what they would think, especially Ginger.

Except, it was Margo who went their first. "Oh, he wants more than just a nanny."

I blinked. "Really? You of all people?"

Ginger scoffed. "Hey, she's got a point. He's paying you essentially a full-time salary for a not-full-time job, *and* he took you to one of the best restaurants in the area."

"Nope," Margo said as she popped the *P*, "he took her to *the* best restaurant in the area. That place is hard to get in to and even harder to return to. They're very stingy about their customer base."

I furrowed my brow. "Really? Because I didn't get that impression. I mean, people were dressed up, sure. But I didn't get the whole 'I'm better than you, so suck it up' vibe. Also, he took his daughter out for dinner. It was convenient for me to come interview because that's where they were, they had the free time, and it gave Gavin a chance to see me in action with his daughter."

"What do you mean, 'in action?'" Ginger asked.

"Something happened, didn't it?" Margo inquired.

I wasn't sure how much I should share, considering that I wouldn't be able to talk too much about their lives after signing whatever non-disclosure agreement Gavin handed me. But I hadn't signed it yet, right? "I don't want to go into too much detail, but his daughter almost had an asthmatic attack at dinner."

Ginger giggled. "And you came to the rescue."

I shrugged. "My brother had asthma growing up. I recognized what was happening and did what I could to help. That's all."

I heard Margo's smile in her tone. "Good for you. I'm glad you're finally getting a little bit of what you deserve."

"I have one more question, though," Ginger said.

I sighed. "Hit me with whatever ridiculousness you've got going on in your head."

She clicked her tongue. "Really? That's how you're gonna do me?"

Margo barked with laughter. "Oh, shut up and ask the question. Because trust me, I'm kind of wondering it, too."

I sat up. "Wondering what?"

The girls fell silent before they both spoke in unison. "Since when are you and Gavin on a first-name basis?"

They fell apart in laughter, and I simply groaned. Maybe the two of them were texting back and forth with one another on the phone call, or perhaps they really were that in sync. I didn't care, though. I was in this for the money and the job opportunity, not to get laid or gawk at some Hollywood actor. Though, it would be hard not to stare at him from time to time.

"So, give us the details," Margo said as her laughter calmed down. "Will you be going back and forth between his place and yours? Staying on the weekends?"

Ginger hopped right back in. "We know he gave Guadalupe's niece the ability to stay overnight if she needed to for anything. But, you know, a married woman and all. She'll never take him up on it."

"Did he give you that option?"

I hesitated to answer, but I did. "Yes, he did. For practical purposes only."

Ginger's excitement grew behind her words. "And will you take him up on it...?"

I felt Margo hanging on to every word as I sighed. "Yes, sometimes. But, only because it'll be more realistic for my sleeping schedule and getting to work at the spa in the morning."

Then, Ginger started in on her bullshit. "Gavin and Eva sittin' in a tree."

"F-U-C-K-I-N-G!" Margo yelled.

"I hate you both," I murmured.

"Hey," Ginger said through her laughter, "just don't let your legs slip and fall open. Rumor has it that's how his ex got pregnant."

I blinked. "Do you know every shred of gossip there is to know in this entire country? Or, do you just make this shit up on the fly and hope it sticks?"

"I mean, I don't know where *you* think babies come from, but that sounds pretty accurate to me," Margo murmured.

I rolled my eyes. "And plus, some Hollywood bigwig won't want anything to do with someone like me. So, can we just stop with the jokes?"

Ginger grew serious really quickly. "Look, I get it. You've never had an ego, and you've never seen how beautiful you really are. But you need to cut that shit out. You're hot as hell, and any man would be lucky if you chose him to sleep with."

"She's right," Margo said, "you're down yourself a lot these days. It breaks my heart when you do it."

I rolled over onto my stomach. "I just pride myself on other things rather than how I look. I'm intelligent. I have common sense. I know how to keep a conversation going. I'm a hard worker. I cook a damn good casserole. I know how to make fresh bread."

"You can bake up a storm," Ginger said.

"And you decorate like a fiend for the holidays. I love that shit," Margo added.

"See?" I asked as I rolled back over. "I've got other things I love about myself. I don't need to start tooting my own horn on how I look, too."

"Well, just know you're gorgeous," Margo said.

"Uh-huh. And Gavin would be lucky as hell to have you if that's what you wanted," Ginger said.

The screen of my phone lit up and caught my eye, so I pulled it away from my face. I put the girls on speakerphone while they chatted back and forth about coming over and helping me pack "go bags" for staying over at Gavin's. I resisted the urge to laugh at them as I navigated to the text that lit up my home screen, but it was from a number I didn't recognize.

"You there, Eva?" Margo asked.

49

"Got a text, hold on," I said mindlessly.

And to my shock, it was from Gavin.

**Gavin: Since tomorrow's Saturday, and you mentioned you don't work weekends at the spa, would you care to get together with Asia and me tomorrow for lunch? It'll give you more time to help the two of you get comfortable.**

A smile tore across my face as I quickly responded, letting him know that I'd be more than happy to accompany them to lunch. I asked him for the time and place, then turned my attention back to my two best friends chatting up a storm without me.

And I was glad, too, that they weren't attempting to add me into the current conversation. I was too busy wrangling the excitement bubbling through my veins.

The last thing I needed to do was get attached like this. Gavin was hot, but he wasn't anything more than that. In fact, he was about to be my boss. So, any issues or lingering lust I had for him had to be tossed out the window come Monday morning. Thankfully, I had the weekend to prepare and clear my head as best as possible. Though, I wasn't sure how much good that would do me.

"Girl, you good?" Ginger asked.

Her voice ripped me out of my trance. "What time is it? I suddenly feel exhausted."

I heard them both shuffling around before Margo cursed. "Fucking hell, it's almost one in the morning."

My eyes widened. "Wait. What?"

Ginger blew a raspberry into the phone. "I needed to be in bed a couple of hours ago. Why do you guys always keep me up with your nonsense?"

Margo and I responded in unison. "Our nonsense?"

Ginger barked with laughter. "Okay, I get how weird that is now."

Margo groaned. "Well, it's time for this old broad to head to bed. And you should enjoy your last weekend of freedom before you start working your life away, Eva."

I decided to keep the weekend plans to myself. "You got that right. I'm heading to bed. I love you guys."

"Love you, too," Ginger said.

"Kiss, kiss," Margo said.

Then, we all hung up the phone, and I lay there, staring at my ceiling, trying my best to fight the excitement crawling through my veins.

## 7

## Gavin

The second I saw Eva walk through the doors of Radcliffe's once again for lunch, a smile spread across my cheeks. She probably thought I was damn-near addicted to this place, and I was, but that was beside the point. The owner of Radcliffe's and I had a silent sort of agreement: I talked up his restaurants and brought new people here as often as I could, and he kept his lips quiet on an ironclad NDA we both had to sign for one another that kept everything in our private lives private.

And while I didn't agree with some of the things he did in his life, so long as he kept up his end of the bargain, we wouldn't have any issues.

"Camila! Hey!" she exclaimed.

The woman I had hired to work with me during the daytime smiled as she got up. I watched the two women embrace in a hug, and it was apparent they knew one another well. I was glad that all of us could sit down in a private room and have a meal together, especially with my daughter here. Asia's comfort was of utmost importance.

I stood. "Eva, thank you so much for coming."

She came over and offered her hand for me to shake, and it caught me off-guard for a split second. I mean, Camila and I had shaken hands, no problem. But, something within me wanted to hug Eva—to pull her close and bury my nose in her beautiful chestnut hair.

"It's not a problem at all. I'm using this weekend to prepare, so I'm glad I get to have a bit more time with Miss Asia before we all jump headfirst into this," Eva said.

I shook her hand a bit longer than necessary, so I dropped it quickly and sat back down. I felt Asia settle on top of my feet as she sat beneath the table, allowing the white tablecloth to shroud her away from the rest of the world. My daughter had forever been shy, which wasn't a good thing when both of her parents were continually in the limelight. Still, I always made sure to carve out safe spaces for her to be herself. Radcliffe's was definitely one of those zones.

It was a safe zone for me, too. Especially in this private room. Why? Well, for one, there were only two entry points: one for guests being escorted by staff and one straight from the kitchen. So, it made the room feel protected. And secondly, there were no windows. That usually made people feel cramped, but for me, it gave me a sense of security. The last thing I needed was paparazzi attempting to climb the roof of this place and snap pictures of me in here, especially with two women at the same time, enjoying lunch with me.

*What a morning headline that would be.*

"Gavin?"

Eva's voice pulled me from the depths of my mind. "Yes?"

Her brow furrowed with genuine worry. "Are you okay? We can do this another time if there's something else that needs you."

I smiled softly at her kindness. "I've always got things on my mind, Eva. But, I promise everything is all right."

Camila dipped beneath the tablecloth. "Oh, that's a pretty picture, Asia."

My daughter giggled. "It's pink, see?"

"It's a glittery pink, too! Where did you get such a pretty color?"

"Eva gave me a pen. She had it in her purse. It's really pretty, and she let me keep it."

I smiled at her from across the table. "I didn't know you let her keep it."

Eva shrugged. "If she can get more use out of it than me, she can have as many as she wants."

Asia gasped as she poked her head out from beyond the tablecloth. "Really? You mean it?"

Eva giggled. "Of course. I'll make sure to come Monday afternoon with all the gel pens I currently have. How's that sound?"

Camila slid back into her chair. "Sounds like I'm the one bringing the water coloring, then."

Asia climbed back up into her chair, joining the crowd. "Yay! I love watercolors and gel pens! Daddy! This is gonna be awesome!"

My head fell back with laughter. "I'm glad you think so, princess. Because I think these two are gonna be a big help."

I felt Camila's smile, but I saw the cool sincerity behind Eva's eyes. Dammit, she had striking eyes. They were the color of a crisp summer day spent running through the woods that were lush with blooms. Her smile reminded me of carefree days lounging around on the beach before my life had taken off into this endless, spiraling abyss of fame and filming schedules.

Her smile made me feel almost... normal again.

"So, I have some questions," Asia said.

I tore my eyes away from Eva's beauty. "Oh? You do?"

My daughter nodded. "Yep. I do. First, Camila. You ready?"

The woman smirked. "Hit me with it."

Asia drew in a deep breath. "Do you like nap times?"

Camila nodded fervently. "Love them. Sleeping is one of my favorite pastimes. And the best naps are taken on a hammock, in my opinion."

My daughter looked up at me. "Daddy, we need a hammock so I can try."

I chuckled. "I can make that happen."

"Eva? You like naps?" she asked.

Eva nodded. "I do, though they make me feel kind of groggy. I'd rather stay up and battle the tiredness before going to bed early and sleeping really late in the morning. Then, I have the excuse to order breakfast in bed!"

My daughter looked up at me and whispered, "They have good answers."

I winked down at her. "It's why I hired them."

She nodded. "All right, next question: cows or bees? And you have to choose their color, too."

Eva blew a raspberry with her lips. "That's simple. Pink bumblebees. They pollinate, so you can grow pretty flowers; they don't sting, so there's no risk there; and who doesn't love pink?"

Asia's eyes darted over to Camila. "What about you?"

Camila playfully considered the question as she thought hard on it, even going so far as to scrunch up her face.

Which made my daughter giggle.

"Brown cows, definitely," Camila said.

Asia blinked. "Brown? That's boring. I don't like boring."

Camila held up her finger. "Ah, but do you like chocolate milk? Because that's definitely how you get chocolate milk."

My daughter gasped. "Daddy, really? Is that true?"

When Eva's laughter erupted from beyond her lips, the sound stopped me in my tracks. It was as if the heavens had opened up and a choir of angels had started singing just for me. The sound washed over me like warm, lazy ocean waves. It reminded me of summers spent with my family up in Myrtle Beach back when I lived a low-key life in the impoverished country hills of South Carolina. It was refreshing and effervescent. It took on a life of its own as she started to snort, and that made everyone laugh just a little bit harder.

It was the most endearing sound I'd ever heard in my life.

*I am so fucked with this woman.*

"Oh my goodness, I'm so sorry," Eva said.

I watched both her and Camila wipe away tears from their eyes as Asia continued rattling off insane questions.

"Jell-O or cotton?"

"Ice cream or marshmallows?"

"Italy or snowball fights?"

The more questions my little girl asked, the more ridiculous their answers became. And soon, all four of us were laughing around the table with our lunches half-eaten and our drinks barely touched. I knew I had made the right decision with these two, and I hoped this was the start of a wonderful dynamic that came together for one common good—helping my daughter become the best version of herself.

*Now, all I have to do is notify Marissa of the changes.*

I wasn't looking forward to that phone call, but it had to happen. It was my responsibility to keep my ex-wife abreast of any dramatic changes in Asia's world, even if she didn't want to give me the same courtesy. I had half a mind to take her to court and get full custody of her, though.

"Crap," Camila murmured.

My head snapped over to her. "Everything okay?"

She stood from her seat. "I'm so sorry to cut this short,

but there's an emergency at the hospital, and it's all hands on deck."

I stood to my feet and held out my hand. "Then, by all means, do what you need to do. Thank you for joining us while you could, and I look forward to seeing you Monday morning."

She quickly shook it. "I appreciate the opportunity, and I'll see you bright and early at six that morning."

Eva stood and gave her a quick hug before Camila rushed out of the room. Then, there were three of us. Asia started slurping her noodles through her lips as I made my way around the table, finally giving in to the gravitational pull I felt between our bodies. I gazed down into her emerald-green eyes as she smiled up at me. I wanted nothing more than to pull her against me and crush our lips together just so I could finally know what she tasted like.

But, I resisted the urge. "If you need to head out as well, please don't feel bad. We accomplished so much more than I thought we would, so you're free to go."

Eva nodded slowly. "I suppose I do have a few things I need to get in line to prepare for Monday."

"Here, let me get someone from the kitchen to watch Asia. I'd like to walk you out to your car."

She shook her head. "No, no. Let Asia eat and hang out here. I can get to my car just fine."

I held my hand out. "Then, let me at least walk you to the exit. It's the least I can do."

"All the way downstairs?"

I pointed to the door leading out of the room. "That door."

She snickered. "That's more like it."

I liked that she didn't want to pull me away from my daughter. With my hand between her shoulder blades, I escorted her over to the door and opened it for her. I ushered her outside and stepped through the threshold, leaving the door just barely cracked open behind me.

And when Eva looked up at me, I felt my gut clench.

"Thank you for taking the time to come to lunch," I managed to spit out.

She licked her lips. "Thank you for letting me come out."

I blinked. "I, uh…"

She shook her head. "No, what I meant was—I just, I just meant thank you for letting—no, that's not right, either. I just meant thanks for the invitation to come and for thinking of me. Platonically, of course. Just—oh, boy."

My smile ached my cheeks as it continued to spread. Eva's eyes fell to her feet, and I watched a blush of embarrassment taint her skin. She had nothing to be uncomfortable about, though. She was the cutest thing I had ever laid eyes on and hearing her stumble over her words only made her more endearing.

*I wish she didn't have to go.* "Let me know when you get home safely."

Her eyes found mine again. "I can do that, of course."

I reached behind me for the door. "And again, thank you

for coming. You'll be at the house around three on Monday, right?"

She nodded. "Right. Three o'clock, sharp."

I stepped back into the room. "Wonderful. I'll see you then."

"See you then, Gavin."

And as I closed the door, putting a physical barrier between the two of us, I felt my own flush creeping its way down the back of my neck.

Though, it certainly wasn't one of embarrassment.

## 8

**Eva**

All night, I couldn't stop thinking about the way Gavin had stared at me yesterday. All through lunch, I had felt his eyes on me, as if he were attempting to peer into my soul. It made me feel exposed but beautiful in an odd way, and I hoped to heaven on high that Camila hadn't caught me staring the way I thought I was at Gavin over lunch. Because if she had, the entire spa would know about it come Monday morning.

Nevertheless, I yawned and stretched my arms above my head. I reached for my phone on my bedside table and noticed I didn't have any missed calls or texts, so maybe I had gotten off scot-free in terms of Guadalupe's niece seeing a little too much. Not that there was much to see. Oh, no. Just a lonely girl, gawking at a Hollywood dreamboat while he onboarded me to be his nanny.

"What a fucking life I lead," I whispered as I set my phone against my chest.

Suddenly, my phone lit up. It started vibrating against my pajama shirt, and I tossed my arm over my face. For a split second, I thought maybe the jig was up. Perhaps it was one of the girls calling to fill me in on my own gossip, or possibly it was Gavin letting me know that he wouldn't be needing my services. Something—anything—to burst my delightful bubble.

I didn't bother seeing who was calling. "Hello?" I asked groggily. "Eva, I know I told you that you wouldn't be working Sundays, but Camila just called out sick."

Once I heard his voice—and the panic inside of it—I bolted upright in my bed. I shook my head. "So much to unpack with that."

"I know it's early, and I'm sure I've woken you up, but I called Camila last night and asked her to work some overtime for me because of a work emergency today. She agreed but then called this morning mid-vomit to tell me—"

I waved my hand in the air and interrupted him, "Weak stomach, sorry. But, I get the point."

He sighed. "I'll make the overtime well worth it. But, I need someone to watch Asia while I'm gone for the day. Can you get here in an hour or so?"

I drew in a sobering breath. "Give me thirty minutes, and I'll be knocking on your door."

"Thank you. Thank you so much."

I nodded. "See you soon."

My mind focused on only one goal as I hung up and tossed the covers off my body—getting to Gavin. He sounded almost frightened. And while I had no idea why, I certainly didn't want his daughter catching the brunt of that insanity. I washed the critical parts of my body down with a washcloth before throwing my hair into a bun. Then I pulled on the comfiest clothes I could find. Thunder boomed in the distance, and the sun was quickly swallowed up by dark clouds forecasting a lovely afternoon of rain and fog to punctuate the weekend. And as I grabbed my to-go bag that I was thankful I had packed the other day, I slipped into some house shoes and booked it out the door, racing to Gavin's to get there within the specified timeframe.

"I'm so sorry for this," he said as he opened my car door, "there's just been a shit-ton of wrenches thrown—"

I held my hand up again before I eased out of the car. "You get going. Let me take care of things here. Any time when you might be home so I can let Asia know?"

He walked me up to the front door. "Sometime around dinner. Six, at the latest."

I walked into his foyer. "All right, sounds good to me. We'll be here!"

"Eva."

My eyes met his. "Yes?"

He smiled softly. "Thank you for this. Really."

I reached out and placed my hand on his shoulder. "Go, Gavin. I've got this."

I watched his body lean in toward mine, and my heart leaped into my throat. Is this man really about to kiss me? I wondered what might happen if he actually did. If those wonderful, impeccable lips that had kissed so many leading ladies might actually want to kiss my own. But, as fleeting as the motion was, his back stood straight again, and he moved away from my touch.

Before waving at me as he jogged off toward his multi-car garage.

*Wheeze.* "D—Daddy?"

I whipped around at the sound of Asia's struggling voice. "Hey there, pretty girl. How are you?"

Her eyes widened as she wheezed again. "Daddy's gone?"

I closed the door and rushed over to her before I scooped her into my arms. "Just for a little bit. But, I promise I won't leave your side. Okay?"

Asia clung to me, and it broke my heart. I felt her chest jumping with a need for air as her wheezing got worse. I walked over to the massive staircase and sat her down, then crouched in front of her and took her hands in mine.

Then, I peered into her panicked eyes. "With me. As slowly as you can. You're safe, Asia. Daddy's gonna be back around dinner, and we'll all share a wonderful meal. We can even cook it ourselves; how does that sound?"

Tears lined her eyes. "Promise?"

I nodded. "Promise, promise."

I walked her through the calming techniques I used in Radcliffe's and had her settled down within a few minutes. Her breathing was still a bit labored, so I tracked down her inhaler in the half-bathroom and gave her a little squirt. Nothing big, just enough to relax her the rest of the way. And when Asia took her first big, unimpeded breath, I smiled.

"So, I have a question."

She looked up at me. "Okay."

I smiled. "How do you feel about snacks and Disney movies?"

Her eyes lit up. "Can we watch Ariel? I love Ariel. She swims a lot."

I giggled. "You like swimming?"

She nodded. "Mhm. When it's not rainy."

"Well, why don't we go into the kitchen, scrounge up some yummy snacks and drinks, then put on some Disney movies? We can cuddle and giggle. Maybe color while we watch after we eat."

"Daddy doesn't let me color on the couch with markers."

I grinned. "What about gel pens?"

Asia took off down the hallway, giggling and yelling to no one in particular about the incredible day we were about to have. And as thunder cracked and lightning flashed, we hunkered down for a lazy Sunday. I turned on Disney+ and put on *The Little Mermaid* while we curled up beneath a rainbow-colored blanket Asia had pulled off her bed. And as we dipped our hands into a massive bowl of caramel-coated popcorn, we played one movie after another.

*Beauty and the Beast.*
*Cinderella.*
*The Princess and the Frog.*
*Brave.*

Then four o'clock rolled around, and it was time to start figuring out dinner.

"So, what do we want to eat in a couple of hours?" I asked.

Asia stretched. "Pizza?"

I gasped. "That is a fantastic idea. But do we want to make it or order it?"

She giggled. "Order it. Then, we can watch another movie."

I pointed at her. "I like your style. What movie do you want to watch before bed?"

She smiled so big, her eyes closed. "My favorite. *Mulan.*"

I gawked. "I thought your favorite was Ariel! My favorite is *Mulan*!"

Asia got up and started jumping on the couch. "Be a man! Be a man! Be a man!"

She jumped into my arms, and I swung her around before we collapsed back against the couch. We turned on the animated version of *Mulan*, and the sweet little girl was so attached to the television that she didn't even register my singing. I shot a text off to Gavin, letting him know about our plans to order pizza for the evening, and when he texted back his order, I wrinkled my nose.

"Ew," I murmured.

"What?" Asia asked.

I peeked down at her. "Your father eats olives on his pizza."

She stuck out her tongue and shook her head, making both of us laugh. This girl really had an outgoing personality once someone was able to peel back those hesitant layers. It hurt my heart to think she had lived so much life that she felt she had to conceal her true self from the world for fear of, well, whatever frightened her. It also made me fall in love with her even more.

*Don't get too attached. Not a good sign.*

Still, we cuddled and enjoyed the movie, and around five, I placed our order. Ham and mushroom for me, grilled chicken and veggies for Gavin, and extra cheese with pineapple for Asia. Complete with dipping sauces, breadsticks, and cinnamon bites for dessert.

However, the delivery guy showed up before Gavin did.

"Where's Daddy?" Asia asked.

I thanked the man for his delivery, tipped him well, and carried the food into the kitchen. "I'm sure he'll be here soon. But, even if he doesn't make it for dinner, guess what?"

She sighed. "What?"

I set all the food onto the kitchen table. "That means we get to eat on the couch and watch another movie."

She gasped. "I never get to eat on the couch! Let's do that."

I bent down. "You have to promise me one thing, though."

"What's that?"

I bopped her nose with my finger. "Make sure to rub it in

Daddy's face in the morning because he'll be eating cold, day-old pizza instead of hot, fresh, cheesy goodness."

She nodded. "I can definitely do that."

Her sentiment made me bark with laughter, and soon we were back on the plush microfiber couch with platefuls of pizza, cups full of soda, and yet another movie on the screen. I hadn't had a day like this in a very long time, and I could tell by how relaxed Asia was beside me that she needed time like this as well.

I made a mental note to team up with Camila to give her one day like this a week. One day to relax and not care about anything in the world.

Around seven o'clock, though, Asia started to yawn. She leaned against me as *Frozen 2* played in the background, but we didn't even get halfway through the movie before her soft snores fell from her precious little lips. I moved her, allowing her to lay against the couch so I could clean things up. And after putting all the dishes into the dishwasher and the pizza into the fridge, I did my best to scoop up Asia so I could walk her upstairs before tucking her in for bed.

"Mmmm, Daddy home?" she mumbled.

I laid her down in bed. "Not just yet. But, I'll send him up here to kiss you when he gets back."

She yawned. "Can I brush my teeth tomorrow?"

I slid her shoes off. "Of course, honey. But, make sure you do it first thing, okay?"

She licked her lips. "Mhm."

I got her shoes and socks off before I slid her comforter

up her body. I tucked her in tightly and handed her a rainbow-colored unicorn stuffed animal she was reaching for. And after a soft kiss on top of her head, I turned off her light and closed her bedroom door behind me.

"Can I sneak in really—"

"Ah!"

Gavin's voice came out of nowhere, and I almost peed myself. I whipped around, my eyes wide as I peered through the darkness of the upstairs. But, no matter how dark it was, I saw his piercing blue eyes staring back at me with something akin to sorrow in his eyes.

"Daddy?" Asia called out.

I stepped off to the side. "I'll be downstairs. Want me to heat you up some pizza?"

He cracked open her door. "More like a glass of wine, if you're offering."

I nodded. "Two glasses of wine, coming up."

It wasn't my job, but the man looked haggard. He slipped into his daughter's room, and I made my way back into the kitchen, where I rummaged around for wine glasses and a nice, strong bottle. However, I couldn't find the wine glasses. All I saw were old sippy cups that had been discarded in a random cabinet, foggy glasses that looked more like tumblers, and coffee mugs.

So, I settled on wine in coffee mugs.

"Asia tells me you two ate on the couch."

I turned around and offered him a mug of wine. "Sorry, all I could find in your cabinets."

He took it and chuckled. "Depending on the day, I don't even bother with glasses. Cheers."

We clinked our mugs together before he leaned against the countertop. And as I studied him, I saw his shoulders slumped a bit. His eyes had bags beneath them as if he hadn't slept in a few days. His legs crossed at his ankles, and he took long pulls of wine until he walked over and topped it off with more of the luscious red I had found in the fridge.

Then, he drew in a deep breath. "How did things go today?"

I sipped my drink and shrugged. "They went well. We had a Disney movie marathon and snacked it up all day."

He snickered. "Sounds like my kind of day."

"Maybe you can join in on the next one."

His eyes met mine. "I'd like that." He set his wine mug off to the side. "Can I ask you something?"

I couldn't read the expression on his face. "Sure, of course. What is it?"

He licked his lips. "Have you ever had one of those days where there's only one thing you can think about doing, but you're not sure what will happen if you do it? But, you know you need to do it in order to end your day on a good note?"

I blinked. "Sure?"

His gaze darkened as his stare connected with mine once more. He pushed off the counter and walked toward me, effectively pinning me into my own little corner. I swallowed hard as he took the mug from my hands. He tossed it back, draining the contents before he set it off to the side.

Then, his hands fell to my waist. "Eva?"

My voice squeaked. "Yes?"

His face came closer to mine. "Tell me to stop."

And when I felt the pulsing of his breath against my lips, I shook my head. "I can't. I'm sorry."

I barely got the phrase out before his mouth connected with mine. My knees went weak as his tongue punched its way through my lips and tangled up with mine. I moaned as his arms cloaked my back. He pulled me away from the countertop and against his body so tightly I could feel his chiseled abs pressing against my soft stomach.

And when we finally came up for air, my pelvis heated with a need for more.

"I can't thank you enough for today," Gavin whispered.

I shook my head quickly. "Seriously, it wasn't an issue. It still isn't, okay? Don't worry about it."

Something passed behind his eyes, and I didn't catch it. And even as his face contorted with it, I still didn't recognize it.

"Why are you looking at me like that?" I asked.

His eyes dropped to my lips. "Like what?"

I drew in a deep breath. "Like... like you want to kiss me again."

His eyes snapped up to mine. "Because I do."

I slid my arms around his neck. "Then, do it."

And before I could blink, his hands gripped my ass cheeks, and he hoisted me onto the kitchen counter and then planted his mouth over mine once more.

## 9

**Gavin**

I couldn't contain myself any longer. Not with Eva. Not with how beautiful she was and how comfortable she made my daughter and how much sunshine she brought into my life. Her walking into a room lit it up, but her smile did something to me that I couldn't deny any longer. During my entire shoot with Jorge, all I thought about was Eva. During every hiccup and every command and every run-through on set, all I thought about was coming home, not just to my daughter, but to her.

And as my hands slid beyond her off-shouldered sweatshirt, I felt her naked skin against my fingertips for the very first time, causing me to growl as my mouth fell against her neck.

"Oh, my God," Eva whispered.

I nibbled against her pulse point as my hands slid up to her tits. Her puckered nipples poked against her bra, and I wanted nothing more than to free them. To release them just so I could lap against her hardened peaks. I needed to stop. I needed to stop being so damn selfish before I ruined something extraordinary that had come into my daughter's life.

But, I couldn't contain myself.

"Shit," she hissed.

I growled against her skin. "I want you so badly."

Her legs spread for me. "Then, take me because I won't tell you to stop."

Something popped inside of me, and I wrapped my arms around her back. I picked her up from the countertop and buried my face into her tits as I walked her into the living room. We fell onto the couch, and food crumbs tumbled everywhere. Our clothes came off in a flurry of passionate need before her legs slid over my shoulders. The smell of her womanhood filled my nostrils. I wanted so desperately to taste her with my tongue until her thighs quivered around my head.

But, my cock leaked with a need that guided me straight to her throbbing entrance before I sank every inch of myself into her precious, beautiful, warm body.

"Oh, fuck," Eva groaned.

I grunted. "Fucking—ah, so tight. Holy hell."

I bent her in half and propped myself up, watching as her face contorted in pleasure. I snapped my hips against hers as her gorgeous curves jumped against my body. And the more I sank into her, the more my day faded away.

With every thrust, I forgot about work.

With every moan, I forgot about that set.

With every kiss, I forgot about the fight I'd had with Marissa in the car coming home.

And with every roll of her hips against my own, she pulled me into her world.

"Gavin. Don't stop. Right there. Oh, shit. Right there. Don't stop. Just like that."

I panted for air as beads of sweat gathered on the nape of my neck. "Come for me, Eva. Do it. Squeeze that dick."

She wrapped her hands around my forearms. "Gavin!"

I captured her lips with my own, silencing her cries of passion. I growled down the back of her throat as she unraveled against me, quaking and milking my cock for all it was worth. That coil in my gut tightened from my toes to my nose, causing my muscles to contract as I sank myself into her pulsing warmth one last time. Then, my body collapsed as my balls pulled up, unleashing my pent-up stress against her walls, coating her as she panted beneath me, her body splayed out for my taking.

I buried my face in the crook of Eva's neck as my cock sat inside of her body. Our intermingled juices pumped out with every pulse of her pussy, but I didn't care. I needed to get the furniture cleaned anyway. I logged the mental note away, for now, knowing damn good and well, it would haunt me until I did something about it.

And as I kissed her skin softly, Eva's voice filled my ear. "Want to talk about it?"

I nuzzled my nose against her jawline. "Ah, won't change anything."

She ran her fingers through my hair. "Might help, though. Always helps me."

I puffed out my cheeks with a sigh and slid from between her legs. No use in having this conversation with us in such a compromising position. I leaned back on my haunches and held out my hand, helping her upright before the two of us leaned against the back of the couch.

*Dammit, she's gorgeous in the moonlight.*

"My ex-wife, Marissa, has already fired Camila."

Her eyes widened. "Wait; what? Why?"

I scoffed. "Why does my ex-wife do anything? Because that's what she felt like at the moment."

"Does she even have that capacity when she didn't even hire us?"

I shrugged. "Not particularly, but Marissa doesn't care. And whatever she said to Camila, it worked. I've called the woman three times today, and nothing I say or offer is making her change her mind."

Eva shook her head slowly. "What in the world does she think you're supposed to do? Is she at least looking for other daytime nannies?"

I chuckled breathlessly. "She's not doing anything. I, however, am trying my best to find someone to help me out during the day. But, there's nothing I can do about it today, so it'll be something I tackle tomorrow."

"Well, I can definitely put in a good word with a few people I know on my end. We'll set the end of next week as a goal, though. You think you can be home during the day for one more week?"

*Already trying to make us a team. I like it.* "Yeah, I think I can swing it."

She smiled. "Then, don't worry. We'll find you another daytime nanny in no time."

I leaned forward, thanking her with a kiss. "I appreciate it so much."

She smiled against my lips. "I also have Tuesday off coming up this week. We have a bunch of servicemen coming in to check on things from top to bottom, so the spa is closed. I could come in all day Tuesday if you'd like. That would give you at least one workday this week where you don't have to worry about things."

I cupped her cheek. "You're outstanding; you know that?"

She blushed. "Just want to help."

*It feels like we've done this for ages.* "Thank you for everything you've already done."

She nodded. "Thank you for giving me a chance."

Then, I pulled her into my arms, settled her against my body as I lay down, and stared up at the ceiling as she curled against me.

Allowing myself a moment's rest not to worry about anything except the beautiful woman lying naked in my arms.

## 10

**Eva**

"Eva?"

I typed away mindlessly on my computer.

"Eva."

I could've sworn I heard my name, but it sounded so far off that I didn't pay it any mind. Until Ginger whipped my chair around, that is.

"Eva!"

I jumped. "Holy shit! What?"

She scoffed. "I've been calling you from the hallway for damn near five minutes. You okay?"

I blinked. "I'm fine. Just got a lot of work. What is it?"

She cocked her head. "No. Something's wrong. What happened?"

Guadalupe stuck her head into my office. "Everyone ready for some good news?"

Thank fuck for distractions. "Yes, ma'am! What's the good news?"

Ginger stood up and pointed at me. "Don't think I'm forgetting about this. I will pull it out of you."

I waved my hand at her. "Come on in, Guadalupe. What's up?"

The older woman rushed into my office and closed the door. "Before I say anything, yes, I do have permission from my niece to share."

"Is this about what happened yesterday?" I asked.

Ginger paused. "What happened yesterday?"

Guadalupe clicked her tongue. "Yesterday couldn't have been any more of a blessing. Camila would have had to quit anyway."

Ginger sighed. "I'm so lost."

I stood to my feet. "Gavin's ex-wife fired Camila yesterday, but Guadalupe's apparently got news that would've forced her to quit the nannying job in the first place. Caught up now?"

Ginger glared at me. "Yeah, got it. Thanks."

Guadalupe clapped her hands. "Camila's pregnant! I'm going to be a tia abuela!"

The sheer shriek that came out of my mouth startled even myself. I loved babies, I loved people having babies, and I loved everything that came with having babies. I lunged myself at Guadalupe and wrapped her up into a great big hug before we started bouncing around and rejoicing. Tears of happiness poured from her eyes onto my shoulder, and I reached out for Ginger, tugging her into a group hug.

"I can't believe it. It's finally happening," Guadalupe whispered.

I kissed the side of her head. "I'm so happy for you."

Ginger rubbed her back. "How far along is she? Do you know?"

Guadalupe released us. "The doctors said that she's right at the beginning, a little less than six weeks along. Just pray for us. Keep us in your thoughts. Camila and her husband have been trying to get pregnant for well over three years now. Let's hope this is their time."

I cupped her hands in mine. "It's definitely their time; you know it is."

But then, Guadalupe paused. "Did you say Camila got fired?"

It took me a while to piece together what she was asking. "Oh! Yes. I know that Gavin's ex-wife fired Camila yesterday. It's why I had to go in all day yesterday and watch Asia."

Guadalupe shook her head. "No, no, no, no. My Camila never gets fired. She called to quit because her morning sickness is catching up with her quickly."

I furrowed my brow. "But, Gavin said—"

Ginger snickered. "Oh, this is gonna be juicy."

I pointed at her. "Everything we say about—or around—Gavin stays here. The last thing we all need is for his private life to be talked about and for the wrong set of ears to hear it. Got it?"

Ginger smirked. "Protective much?"

Guadalupe giggled. "Seems like she likes him."

I rolled my eyes. "Promise me. Right now. Both of you."

Ginger shrugged. "I'm not that bad with shit like that."

Guadalupe held up her hands in mock surrender. "As God as my witness."

I nodded. "Good. So, why would Camila call his ex-wife to quit if Gavin were the one who hired her? That doesn't make any sense."

Guadalupe sighed. "All she told me was that she couldn't get Gavin to pick up, so she called his ex-wife. Maybe she thought the woman could get in touch with Gavin or something."

Why would she lie about something like that, though? What's the point?

"Anyway," Ginger said as she put her hands on her hips, "this calls for a celebration, especially since the spa is being serviced tomorrow. How do you guys feel about cake?"

I clapped my hands. "And celebratory discounts for members! Let's get them in on this. Flash sale, all day today. All services, products, and add-ons are thirty percent off."

Guadalupe clapped my shoulder. "I think you two have got this, so I'm going to go grocery shopping. I'll get cake, a vegetable and fruit platter, some refreshments for us to enjoy. It'll be wonderful."

Ginger scurried to my door. "I'll tell Margo out front to start applying the discounts!"

The spa erupted into one massive celebration for Camila

and her new addition to her family. Margo put up streamers and balloons she found in the back storage room, and Guadalupe came in with bags filled to the brim with cups, ice, sodas, juices, finger foods, and all sorts of sweet treats. Our customers celebrated with us and rejoiced in happiness while reveling in their discounts. Our stock flew off the shelves so quickly that we had to restock not once but three separate times that day.

But, no amount of celebration wiped my mind of my memories.

I have to talk with Gavin about what happened between us.

I clocked out right at two in the afternoon and blazed a trail to his place. Not only did I want to tell him the good news about Camila, but I also needed to tell him about the lie his ex-wife had spewed. Part of me thought it wasn't my place, but the other part of me felt Gavin had a right to know. He seemed so stressed that his ex had just swept in and terminated someone without his knowledge, and I didn't want that hanging over his head any longer.

If he's going to torture himself, it might as well be with the truth.

I pulled up to the house and really stopped to take a look at it. The crisp, clean white exterior was dotted with bright-yellow shutters, giving the place a very summery sort of feel. The columns attached to the wrap-around porch were unlike anything architecturally seen in this area, and I knew it had to have come from nowhere else except Gavin's upbringing. I smiled at the idea of baby Gavin being raised in a house similar to this one. Beautiful plantation-style columns and running around playing tag on the porch while his parents and grandparents rocked the day away in rocking chairs fit for kings and queens.

But, a stark knock on my window pulled me from my trance. And I saw a stoic Gavin standing on the other side.

"I gotta go. Asia's inside," he said through the glass.

I opened the door and slipped out, but he was already booking it toward the garage.

"I have something to tell you!" I called out after him.

He held a thumbs up in the air. "We'll talk soon, then!"

And like a lightning bolt, he was gone. No kiss. No acknowledgment of what had happened last night. Not even a hug. Just him, a command, and then an empty space before I felt my heart sink to my toes.

"It's okay. Daddy does that sometimes when he's upset," Asia said.

I felt her hand slip into mine, and I looked down at her. "Any idea why he's upset?"

She shrugged. "Usually, it's Mom. I heard them yelling this morning."

I crouched down as the garage opened off in the distance. "Well, why don't we go inside and find something fun to do, yeah?"

She nodded with a smile. "I like that idea. Can we paint? I like painting."

"Of course, we can. And then, we can figure out what to—"

The peeling away of tires interrupted my statement before smoke kicked up into the air. I stood up and whipped around, catching the backend of Gavin's canary-yellow sports car as it tore down the driveway. I heard his tires squealing as he hit the road, trying his hardest to get out of here as quickly as he could. I wasn't sure what had him in such a rush, but something told me I didn't want to be around when he got home.

"Come on, pretty girl. Let's go find something to paint," I said.

I led her back inside, but I was only partially there. I kept racking my mind as to what I could've done to make Gavin treat me so coldly. Last night had been phenomenal. A bit awkward, maybe, but still amazing. And today, it felt like he wanted nothing to do with me. But, once Asia and I started painting, a text rolled through my phone, and it made me feel a little more comfortable with things.

Gavin: I'm sorry for being in such a hurry, but I had to be on set earlier than I thought.

I quickly texted him back while Asia hogged all the paint colors.

Me: Thank you for messaging. And I totally get that, no worries. But, I did figure out something I thought you should know.

Those three little dots started bouncing before his reply popped up.

Gavin: Oh? What happened?

I sighed before I started in on the message.

Me: I saw Camila's aunt at work today, and she informed me that Camila is pregnant. That's why she quit; she wasn't terminated. I just wanted to let you know that your ex-wife didn't fire anyone, that's all.

I expected him to start typing back, but it didn't happen. I expected him to be relieved or even tell me that he figured something like that might have occurred. But, there was nothing. I sent my message, I saw the little D change to an R, telling me he had read the text, but then, nothing happened.

No little dots bounced.

No message came through.

It was as if he read the message and decided it wasn't worth a response.

Maybe I shouldn't have told him.

"Look, Miss Eva! Look!"

Asia's voice pulled my eyes to her paper, and I saw what appeared to be a beautiful sunset. The bottom half of the page was blue, and there were little hills at the top that almost looked like waves. And the top half of the paper had a massive yellow ball up at the corner with pinks and purples and blues streaking across the sky.

"It's beautiful. I love it," I said.

She looked up at me with a smile. "You can have it if you want."

I smiled. "I'll put it front and center on my refrigerator at home."

Her eyes grew determined. "Well, in that case, let me add

some fishes and my name. Painters always sign their names to stuff."

I giggled. "Sounds like a plan, pretty girl."

But as the day passed on, bleeding into another dinner Asia and I planned together, I never got a response from Gavin. Not a phone call, or an email, or even a text message, letting me know what time he'd be home. And it made me wonder if I had ruined everything between us in one sweeping text message.

## 11

## Gavin

The second I read Eva's message, I had to put my phone down. Anger, unlike anything I had ever experienced, pooled in my gut, and I had to leave Jorge's set in order to get some fresh air. I burst through the security guards just outside the door and heard people scrambling to get their cameras. I slipped into a darkened alcove before one of the bodyguards stood in front of me, blocking the flashing of cameras and muting the onslaught of questions as people tried to pry quotes from my dying lips.

Why on God's great green earth would Marissa lie about something so stupid?

Did she not feel she had enough control over my life? Did she want to feel more powerful? More in tune with Asia's life? Well, she needed to be around to have those privileges, for starters. But what did I know? I was simply "the man who knocked her up."

"Gavin out here?" Jorge exclaimed.

I sighed as his voice resonated in my ears. "Yeah, I'm out here."

He pushed his way through the security guards. "You want to get back inside so my set can no longer be a madhouse? They love you, you know."

I scoffed. "Wish Marissa loved her daughter as much."

He gripped my arm. "Let's get you inside before the wrong set of ears hears that shit."

Jorge dragged me back inside before promptly dismissing the set for a late lunch. But, I knew he wasn't finished with me yet. He kept pulling me across the damned place until we were behind his office door. And after yelling at his assistant to get us both some lunch, he closed us in.

"All right, spill. What did she do now?"

I snickered as Jorge turned to face me. "That obvious?"

"It's always obvious when she does something. What did Marissa do now?"

I shook my head slowly. "Well, you know she fired Camila, right?"

He blinked. "Right."

I raked my hands through my hair. "According to Eva, who heard it from Camila's aunt, she didn't get fired. Camila quit because she's pregnant."

Jorge's eyes widened. "I mean, congrats to her. But, why the fuck would your ex lie about something so stupid?"

My arms flopped to my sides. "Beats the fuck out of me! Why would she even lie about something like that? None of this is sitting right with me. The quick elongation of her work contract. Her lying about firing Camila when she really quit. She's up to something; I know she is."

"Maybe she wants you back, so she's eliminating all of the women you've surrounded yourself with."

I shot him a look. "I would rather die."

He leaned against the wall. "You don't look any more relieved than you did a few minutes ago."

"I'll be relieved when I have answers. And a new daytime nanny."

"Everything going okay with Eva, though?"

I paused for a bit too long. "Sure, yeah. Why?"

He narrowed his eyes. "Gavin?"

"What."

He pushed off the wall. "Is everything actually okay with Eva?"

I shrugged. "Yeah. She's great with Asia. She's generally nice to have around."

"But...?"

I sighed. "I wish I could employ your full-time. That would solve all of my issues in one fell swoop. But, she's still got that job at the spa, and I can't ask her to quit and come work for me, can I?"

He blinked a few times. "Not what I was getting at, but okay. I'll play your game."

"What game?"

He waved his hand in the air dismissively. "Yes, you could always ask Eva to quit. Especially if you can make up the difference in what her paychecks would be. Why wouldn't you be able to at least ask?"

I knew there was something else on his mind, but I let it fly over my head. "Because it's rude, for starters."

"If you want to look at this from purely a practical standpoint, here it is. You could pay her in one job what she can't even make with two. You could pay her more than that spa ever could, no offense to Guadalupe or Yuslan. So, what do you get by not even proposing the idea?"

I chewed on the inside of my cheek. "You do have a point."

He put his hand on my shoulder. "The worst Eva can say is no, dude. You're not asking her to marry you or some shit; you're just asking her to consider working for you full-time. Employers poach employees with incentives all the time. Just think of it as another business transaction."

And while I knew it was more complicated than that between the two of us, I didn't dare let Jorge know that. He was just as bad with gossiping as any woman I'd ever come across, and I knew rumors of my love life would be halfway across the city by nightfall if I mentioned anything.

The idea of having Eva around more did sound fantastic, though.

"Let me shoot her a quick text," I said.

He smiled and squeezed my shoulder. "'Atta, boy. Just tell her you want to talk with her tonight and that it's nothing bad. Then, let's inhale the food I smell coming down the hallway because I'm starving."

I chuckled as I typed away at my message. "Sounds like a plan."

**Me: Hey. Sorry for the drop-off. Pretty busy here on set. Listen, do you have time to talk tonight before you head out? I have some changes in the babysitting schedule I want to speak with you about.**

I didn't expect as prompt of a response as I got, but as Jorge took our food from his assistant and started setting it up, I watched those three little dots bounce before her message popped up.

**Eva: I'm sorry if I contributed to how busy things are. And I'll definitely make the time. See you when you get here.**

I wanted to text back, but I wasn't sure what to say. So, I simply sent a thumbs-up emoji before closing out the message. It seemed so informal, but what else was there? A heart? A winky face? Did penis and panting emojis exist?

"You gonna eat or what?" Jorge asked.

I slid my phone into my pocket and sat down. "Thanks for lunch."

He shrugged. "Anytime. You usually buy anyway. Nice to know I can treat you every once in a while."

As I picked up the carton of lo mein noodles, I set my

sights on tonight. I had to find the right words and come in hot with a monetary deal; otherwise, I risked her saying no. And I really didn't want her to say anything other than yes. She was a joy to have around. Asia wouldn't stop talking about their time together. Having a singular nanny that came regularly would provide my daughter with the stability she didn't get from myself or her own damn mother.

I just had to do everything in my power to get Eva to play on my side.

The rest of the day soared by, and when I got home, it was damn near nine o'clock. It had been a late day with even later meals, and I wolfed down a chicken wrap as I drove home. I hated making Eva wait as long as she had. Asia had been in bed for over an hour, and I could only imagine how long Eva had been twiddling her thumbs, waiting for me to get back.

When I walked through the front doors, however, I didn't find an angry woman. I didn't find anyone harrumphing or sighing because I was late. I didn't find a scowl or a slew of questions as to where I had been.

Instead, I found Eva at the other end of the foyer, standing there with two coffee mugs filled with wine I could smell from the front door.

And with the coolness of an introverted high school nerd with much too big of a crush, I blurted the words out before I even closed the front door behind me. "How much would it take for you to quit your job at the spa and be a full-time, live-in nanny?"

## 12

**Eva**

I blinked. "Sorry, what was that?"

Gavin closed the front door and locked it before he strode across the foyer toward me. His blue eyes held mine captive as his blond hair shuffled against his forehead. He looked positively exhausted, but the intensity and the passion of his words portrayed a very different scenario.

He plucked his coffee mug filled with wine before he ushered me down the hallway. "Let's sit and talk. I had a whole spiel planned before that question," he said with a chuckle.

I gave him a polite giggle, but his question kept tumbling around in my mind. Was this the "change in the babysitting schedule" he was talking about?

Did he really just ask me to name my price?

"Here. Sit," Gavin said.

He pulled out a chair for me at the kitchen table, and I eased myself into it. I watched him walk around and sit in front of me, his feet promptly settling against my own. I felt his warmth trickling slowly up my legs, but I tried to keep my wits about me as he drew in a deep breath through his nose.

Then, he launched into his spiel. "So, Asia can't stop talking about you."

I smiled softly. "I'm glad. She's a great girl."

"And you're great with her. I've never seen Asia so happy and so outgoing around another person. You've really done a number on her."

Just her? "She's special to me, too."

He leaned forward. "Which is why you're perfect for being her nanny. All of this 'daytime evening time' shit is just unstable for her. She struggles so much with change, and she's endured so much of it in the seven years she's been alive. Having one person here from the time she wakes up until the time she goes to bed will always be the best equation for her. And if we can work something out like that, then I can give you a plethora of incentives and options I'm sure you don't get at the spa."

What's the harm in hearing him out? "Like... what?"

He leaned back against his chair and sipped his wine. "For starters, you name your price, and you've got it."

"I'm still thinking about it. What else?"

"Weekends off and holidays. It'd be a strictly Monday

through Friday job, with your weekends only being taken up by an emergency of some sort. I have no issues toggling my filming schedule around something like that, oh! And you'll need a passport. If you don't have one, I'll pay for it."

I blinked. "A passport? Why?"

He grinned. "Asia loves traveling. We take one major trip a year, and I know she'll want you to come along. We can work it out later on, but if you choose not to come, you'd be on paid leave, and if you chose to come, I'd not only continue paying you for being with us, but I'd pay for your trip."

My eyebrows rose. "That's very generous of you. Thank you."

"You'd also get your pick of any room in the house. Or, you could set up in the guesthouse and have your own little housing space. I'll make a space for you in the garage to put your car, you'd have free rein of the house, whether or not we're here, and I wouldn't charge you rent."

I gawked. "No rent? Why not?"

He took a long pull from his wine. "Because the favor you'd be doing me far surpasses a monetary value like rent. Plus, it's not like the bills are going to skyrocket with you here."

My mind swirled with so many things. "What about health insurance? I've got a very basic plan through the spa, but it's almost worthless."

And he had a quick answer to my question. "Since you'd be living here and I'd be paying for your housing and utilities,

I could technically put you on an added plan to mine and Asia's health insurance policy. That isn't an issue at all."

"Would it have coverage for yearly check-ups and stuff like that?"

He nodded. "Dental, vision, ER. It'd be comprehensive medical insurance, and it would be one of the best private plans out there."

"How much would that be a month? And don't tell me 'nothing' if you're already not charging me for rent or food or utilities. There has to be something I contribute to."

He chuckled. "If you insist, your 'employee' side would probably be around nine hundred or so a month."

I tried not to choke on my own tongue. "Fair enough."

"But, I really don't mind pay—"

I held up my hand, silencing his words. I had so many things rushing through my head that I wasn't sure where to begin. For starters, could I really abandon Guadalupe and Yuslan at the spa? I mean, they had given me my start. I owed a lot of my life to the paycheck they afforded me. It almost felt like betraying them, in a way, if I quit and jumped ship. But, on the other hand, my student loans would already be crushing enough. And if I could find a way to make enough money to double-up on those payments and get out of my rundown apartment in the process, they'd be happy for me, right?"

Just throw out a number. What do you have to lose?

So, I went with the first figure that popped into my mind. A figure he probably wouldn't be able to fulfill.

"If I'm going to be living here—which means I'll always be on-call—and if my responsibilities don't stop after a certain time—you know, if Asia has an attack in the middle of the night or something—I'd say eight grand is a fair place to—"

"Done."

I felt my face pale. "What?"

He held out his hand. "Eight grand a month, paid in halves on the first and the fifteenth, and I'll foot the bill on whatever has to happen to cut your lease at your place. Deal?"

My eyes fell to his outstretched hand. "I mean, I still have to notify my bosses."

He wiggled his fingers. "They can't deny a two-week notice if you really want to put it in."

I swallowed hard. "And everything we talked about stands?"

He nodded. "You have my word, Eva."

I knew this was a bad idea. I didn't need to shake his hand. The spa was safe. The spa was my home. The spa didn't have beautiful Hollywood men with chiseled abs and tailored pecs walking around with deadly smiles while they slung dick around that made me salivate.

But I watched as my hand gravitated to his before I shook it. "Then, it's a deal," I said.

The look of relief that washed over Gavin's face reinforced the fact that I had made a good decision. I just didn't know if it was a wise one. And now, I had to go to work tomorrow morning with the intent of speaking with Guadalupe about resigning—a conversation I never thought I'd have after they had embraced me like one of their own.

I dropped his hand. "Actually, can this be a hesitant 'yes?'"

He grabbed his coffee mug. "Don't worry; I'm not under the impression that you're quitting tomorrow."

"I just—Guadalupe and Yuslan, the owners, are like family to me. I don't just want to spring this on them. I want to make sure they're going to be okay with me gone first."

"Trust me, when it comes to family, I completely understand. I'll need a solid confirmation by Friday so I can make other arrangements if you don't want the job. But, take your time up until that point."

"Thank you, Gavin. For your offer, for even considering such a salary, and for your generosity in general. I feel like just the words aren't nearly enough."

He grinned. "I'm sure there are other ways you'll find to thank me in time."

I felt a flush creep up into my cheeks before his eyes widened.

"Eva, that came out so wrong. I shouldn't have even said it in the first place. It just kind of—"

I stood to my feet. "What was that?"

He looked up at me. "I just—I'm sorry for how those words—"

I planted my hands onto the table and leaned over, accenting my cleavage. "Sorry, I can't hear you. What was that, sir?"

I purred that last word to the best of my ability, and his

eyes fell to my tits. I saw his jawline clench as my heart rate skyrocketed, but when I saw that telltale flush creep down his neck, I knew I had him. Those words came soaring out, and they quickly stoked a heat I had been abating in my gut all damn day. And now, I had an opening I wanted more than anything to take.

"Eva, you don't have—"

I walked around the table, letting my fingertips slide against the distressed wooden top. "I don't have to what, sir?"

He turned in his chair, his eyes raking up and down my body. "You don't, uh, just—wh—what?"

I sank to my knees in front of him. "Cat got your tongue?"

His breathing ticked up a notch. "Has anyone ever told you that your eyes sparkle like emeralds?"

I giggled as my hands slid up his shins. "Yes."

"Have they ever told you that they're one of your more gorgeous features?"

I fluttered my eyelashes at him as my hands crept against his knees. "Yes."

His eyes darkened. "Then, has anyone ever told you that they'd look better peeking up from between a pair of thighs?"

I pressed his knees open before I reached for his belt buckle. "Now, that's a first, sir."

I stripped him of his belt and quickly unbuttoned his pants. He reached in and pulled his cock out for me, stroking it as his girth leaked from the tip. I licked my lips as I shuffled between his legs, allowing my hands to slide around his body.

Then, after he bounced it against my lower lip, I sucked it into my mouth.

"Holy fuck," he groaned.

I watched his head fall back as I licked his precum off his skin. I slid him back as far as I could before I wrapped my hand around the base of his cock. I hollowed out my cheeks, slowly pulling my lips up as he jolted and bucked his hips. And as I felt the veins of his cock bulging against my tongue, I wrapped it around the head of his dick, quickly sucking him to the back of my throat.

"Jesus fuck, Eva. Just like that."

His hand gripped the tendrils of my hair, and I moaned around his thickness. I cupped his balls with my free hand and felt my spit already dripping down his length. I bobbed my head with his movements as he tugged my hair and pushed my head down, following a pattern and a rhythm that made me wanton for more. I felt my panties wetting—my pussy pounding. The taste of him alone made my eyes roll back as he commanded my movements. But, it wasn't until he ripped me off his cock and pulled me up that I popped inside. That I felt a desperate need to have him, no matter the consequences.

And as he stood to his feet, carrying me with him, I allowed him to manipulate my body until I was lying on my back against the kitchen table with his hands already pawing to get my pants off.

## 13

**Gavin**

I pulled her shoes off and tossed them onto the floor before tugging at her leggings. Eva giggled and wiggled around as they fell off to the side, crumbling to the floor in a small pile. I wrapped my arms behind her legs and pulled her to the edge of the table, taking pride in how she squealed for me as I slid her wet panties to the side.

And as our eyes locked, I slowly sank into her until her eyes fluttered closed involuntarily.

"Oh, shit," she moaned.

I grunted as I sank into her tight, wet depths. "Man, oh man, you will get addicting."

She cupped her breasts. "As if I'm not already addicted to you."

Her words filled me with fire. "Then, hang on for the ride, beautiful."

She locked her legs around my back, and I pulled my hips back. I slammed into her, feeling her essence slowly trickle down my balls as her back arched. She clawed at the kitchen table, knocking off her coffee mug of wine that went crashing to the floor. And as the liquid splattered all over my marble floor, I kept my eyes locked with her.

Locked with the flush of her skin.

Locked with the bouncing of her tits.

Locked with the sight of my cock disappearing into her pussy.

I couldn't get enough of her.

If she says "yes," we're making this a regular thing.

"Gavin," she groaned.

My hands planted onto the kitchen table as I hovered over her. I rocked against her, grinding my tightly wound curls against her swollen clit. Her eyes bulged as her hands slid up my arms, then she raked her nails down my skin, a sensation that shivered me to my core and made my dick grow thicker against her walls.

"Shit, shit, shit, shit," she hissed.

I growled with every thrust I managed. "Goddammit, Eva, you feel amazing."

She bucked ravenously against me, her pussy hungry for more as the sounds of wet skin slapping wet skin filled the air. My balls pulled up as her walls collapsed around my cock, sending her into a spiraled frenzy of lust and carnal desire.

Her jaw unhinged in silent pleasure before I covered her mouth with my own, swallowing her sounds down until there was nothing left. And with one last pump of my hips, my dick finally exploded.

I grunted down the back of her throat while her tongue danced the tango with my own. I curled my fingertips into the top of the table, rutting against her like a wild fucking animal. Stream after stream of arousal shot from the tip of my girth, filling her to the brim before the evidence of our debauchery spilled onto the table beneath us.

I resisted the urge to collapse on top of her while she panted, and instead, I gazed into the post-coital bliss Eva's eyes afforded me.

And I knew I was in trouble in all the best ways.

I kissed her lips softly. "My shower is yours if you'd like it."

She shook her head slowly. "Might just get into more trouble there."

I winked. "A woman after my own heart."

She giggled, and the blush that colored her cheeks became my favorite color in the entire world. It suited her so well, and I wanted to keep providing that for her for all the days she lived with me. But, the moment burst the second she sat up, and my cock fell from between her legs.

"I should head home and get some rest for tomorrow. The morning will be here before we know it."

I backed away and pulled my clothes up my legs. "You've got a point."

She quickly got dressed as well. "I'll see you as soon as I can get off work?"

I nodded. "I'm looking forward to it."

We side-stepped the spilled wine and had a small moment of laughter together. I ushered Eva to the front door with my hand on the small of her back, and I could've sworn I felt her lean against my palm just a little bit harder than usual. I buried my grin as I opened the door. I escorted her out to her car and briefly wondered if she'd accept a "business vehicle" from me. Her car looked like it was on half of its last leg.

"If you want to stay, I can always have Lucas drive you to work tomorrow," I said.

She opened her car door. "I really should be getting home. I need a shower and some time to think about how to break things to Guadalupe and Yuslan."

I nodded as I held onto her door. "Of course. I understand."

She sank into her seat. "Thank you."

I bent forward. "And if you do decide to take me up on that job offer, we're going to see about getting you a vehicle for business purposes. If you're going to be driving my little girl around, you'll be doing it in something that looks a bit safer than this car."

She gawked. "I could just use one of yours. I'm sure you've got—what?—five or six?"

I grinned. "But, this one would be yours. Think it over. It comes with the package."

The look of shock that rolled over her features filled me

with such pride that my chest puffed out. I liked that look on her face. I liked the fact that I could shock her and impress her at the drop of a hat. And I hoped with all my might that she'd give me the chance to continue to surprise her and sweep her off her feet every time she turned around.

She just had to take the job first.

I tapped the hood of her car before I backed away, sliding my hands into my pockets. I fiddled with some lint trapped down in the corner because I knew that if I didn't give myself something to do, I'd chase her all the way to the end of the drive and haul her ass back up to my bedroom with her body hoisted over my shoulder. I drew in deep breaths as I watched her car slip off down the driveway and quickly disappear out of sight.

Then, as I turned to head back inside, a thought crossed my mind. A thought that had me scrambling for my cell phone.

"Hey! Gavin! Long time, no talk. How are things?" Trey asked.

I locked up the house for the night. "Things are, well…"

He chuckled. "That good, huh?"

I looked at the massive pile of splashed wine and sighed. "I kind of have a favor to ask."

"Well, ask and ye shall receive if I can help out! What's on your mind?"

"I know you usually book out your yachts weeks in advance, but I was kind of hoping you had something I could rent for the weekend?"

"Ah, you want to have some fun on the water with someone special?"

"More like two special people. Asia and Eva."

I heard his smirk through the phone. "And who's Eva?"

I started searching for a mop. "The woman that I'm hoping will agree to be Asia's nanny. I'm expecting a positive answer from her by Friday, so I was hoping to book us a little trip so the three of us can get to know one another better."

He barked with laughter. "And you really expect me to believe that?"

"I'm hoping you will simply because it's damn near eleven, and I've been up since five."

"Well, you're in luck. We had a cancellation this morning on one of our bigger yachts due to sickness running through the family."

I finally located the mop and pulled it out of the pantry. "Great. Whatever I need to do to secure that for this weekend, just use my card you have on file."

"Any sort of monetary limit for beverages and food?"

"Just make sure it's top-shelf stuff. You know Asia loves that freshly-squeezed apple juice."

He snickered. "And I'm really supposed to believe you're rolling out the red carpet for a soon-to-be nanny that hasn't even given you a 'yes' yet?"

I ran the mop across the floor. "Just do it, would you?"

He laughed so hard he started wheezing. "Fine, fine. All right. You know the drill. You'll see the charges, you've got twenty-four hours to change something, and I'll see you guys Friday at four!"

And as I finalized everything with Trey on the phone, only one thought crossed my mind as I cleaned up the wine and made my way upstairs.

I really hope Eva quits that damn job.

## 14

**Eva**

I couldn't wait until work. I had to speak with them now about the issue that had arisen with Gavin. So, the second I left his place, I headed straight for Guadalupe's. It was late, and I wasn't sure if they'd be up. But, this couldn't wait until morning.

I'd never get any sleep if I let it wait that long.

I pulled into their driveway around eleven-thirty and sighed. Guilt filled my gut as I opened my car door and headed for the alleyway to get to their front door. Guadalupe and Yuslan's place was situated a bit differently. Still, it lent itself to a beautiful backyard setup that they had. Their front door was actually in a widened alleyway. Their home itself was a once-abandoned building with connected brick townhomes that had long since been neglected. They had purchased the property for pennies on the dollar—or so Yuslan had told me one day—and they had used the money from their spa to renovate the entire place.

Now, they rented out three of the townhomes and lived in the corner one. The one with the largest backyard.

I stood on their "porch" and drew in a deep breath. But, when I raised my knuckles to knock on the door, Yuslan whipped it open. He gestured for me to come in without a word spoken, and I stepped through the threshold, breathing in the wonderful smell of tamales and tea.

"Got some food for you!" Guadalupe exclaimed.

I navigated my way into the kitchen. "You're up cooking this late?"

Yuslan pulled out a chair for me at the table, and I thanked him before sitting. Guadalupe didn't answer my question as she set a plate of tamales onto the table. Her husband gathered condiments for the fresh hot tea as well as the food in front of us. Rice came off the stove, and vegetables came out of the oven. It was a fucking feast at damn near midnight, and I wondered if they had already been up or if they were putting on a show because they saw me pull up.

Then, they both sat down with me and started dishing up food.

"So, what's on your mind?" Guadalupe asked.

I shrugged. "Just a lot of stuff."

Yuslan filled my plate with food before handing me a fork.

So, I took it and had a few bites while Guadalupe continued with her line of questioning.

"You drive from his place here?" she asked.

I snickered. "That obvious?"

She smiled. "Is the new job going okay?"

I felt my gut clench. "It's going really well, actually. I really like it."

"*Bueno*! Wonderful. That is so good to hear, Eva."

"He's a wonderful father, Guadalupe. And devoted to his career. He just needs help, you know? Nothing wrong with that."

She shook her head. "Nothing wrong with that at all."

"And besides, it's not like I wouldn't be around. I'd come to visit just as often as I'm there now. I mean, I'd still be a member at the spa, and I need those facials Yuslan does. I don't know what he uses, but they're outstanding."

She cocked her head. "You're talking as if you're not coming back to the spa."

And when I paused, Yuslan's voice filled the air. "He's asked you to work full-time for him, hasn't he?"

My eyes didn't waver from Guadalupe's. "Yes. He has."

She reached out and took my hand. "And you like the job?"

I nodded. "I really do. He's willing to pay me a full-time salary to do it as well. He's offered to move me in and not charge me rent. He's even willing to put me on his and his daughter's health insurance. It's—it's the perfect plan, you know?"

Guadalupe squeezed my hand. "I think it sounds like the perfect position for you, then."

I felt shellshocked until Yuslan spoke.

"Sounds like you've found your *alto, oscuro, y guapo*. Eh?"

Guadalupe started laughing as my jaw dropped open. I slowly looked over at him to find him smirking at me, and I tried to rack my brain for the last time I had seen Yuslan do anything but be stoic and keep quiet.

"Thank you for stealing my line, *cariño*," Guadalupe said through her giggles.

I shook my head. "So, you're not upset?"

Her eyes returned back to mine. "We make jokes, but it's also true. It sounds like you've found your man. Where you're supposed to be. And if that's the case, then you need to go get him. You need to be at his side if he's the one for you."

I snickered. "We're talking about a job, Gee. Not marriage."

Yuslan shrugged. "Same difference, in our opinion."

I scoffed in disbelief, but deep down, I wondered if the two of them were right. I mean, they'd been right with both Margo and Ginger. So, why couldn't they be right now?

The thought filled me with a giddy sort of excitement, and I was suddenly hungry for everything sitting in front of me. I pulled away from Guadalupe touch, and I reached for my tea, ready to sip on it and let my thoughts swirl around in my head for a little while. We ate in silence as I turned things over, weighing the pros and cons before ultimately coming to a decision.

So, my stare gravitated back to Guadalupe. "Guadalupe?"

She swallowed her food and smirked. "Yes, Eva?"

I drew in a deep breath. "I'm officially putting in my two-week notice."

She smiled brightly. "I've never been so happy to accept one in all my life."

Yuslan butted in. "She's also putting in two weeks' worth of vacation."

My head snapped toward him. "Wait; what?"

He leaned forward, his eyes locking with my own. "It's so you can start ASAP. You know you're supposed to be there. So, no use in delaying."

I didn't know what to say. I didn't know what to do. So, I launched myself at Yuslan and wrapped my arms around his neck. He chuckled as he stood, taking me with him before he patted my back with his hands. Then, I released him and walked around the table so I could hug Guadalupe as well.

"I'm gonna miss you guys so much," I whispered.

She giggled softly against my ear. "We'll keep your membership status, complete with the discount you get for being an employee. So long as you promise to use it and come see us often."

I kissed her cheek. "I'll come every week, I promise."

She rubbed my back. "Good. Good, good."

The hug lingered for a little bit longer before I excused myself from the table. I reached over and snatched one last bite of my tamale before I made my way into their bathroom. I didn't want to make Gavin wait for another second longer on my decision because I knew he was walking on pins and needles. And I didn't want him to have to battle that while he was at work all week.

I closed myself in the bathroom and leaned against the counter. I smiled as I pulled my phone out of my back pocket and opened up my text messages to Gavin. My fingers typed away as I formulated the exact right way to break the good news to him, then shot the message off.

And almost instantly, it was read, and those three little dots were bouncing up and down.

**Gavin: Really? Are you going to take the job?**

I smiled as my fingers clicked back as quickly as possible.

**Me: Yep. I'm with Guadalupe and Yuslan right now. I just put in my two-week notice as well as a two-week paid vacation. I can start whenever you need me.**

**Gavin: So, you could technically get over here tomorrow morning?**

**Me: I'd need serious help moving since that won't give me much time to pack. But, yes. That technically means I could come in tomorrow.**

Gavin read the message, but those little dots didn't start bouncing. So, I tucked my phone back into my pocket and splashed some water on my face. My stomach growled with a need for the food out in the kitchen, so I dabbed my face off and gazed at myself in the mirror.

"I'm Gavin Lincoln's full-time nanny," I whispered. And the sentiment alone spread a smile so big across my cheeks that my jawline started to ache.

Nevertheless, I eased myself out of the bathroom and started back for the kitchen. I felt my phone vibrate in my back pocket, but I figured I could check it once I finished eating. The big news had been dropped, Gavin knew I was taking the job, and that's all that was necessary until I got home.

Then, after finishing my food, Guadalupe and Yuslan packed me a massive to-go tray before I headed home. I walked into my apartment and promptly made my way into the kitchen. I wanted to take that food with me tomorrow and have Asia try some of it because I knew she'd love it. I stuck it in the fridge and gazed out across my small, one-bedroom apartment, and smiled at the idea that I'd never have to come back to this place ever again.

*I have to email my landlord.*

I rushed into my bedroom and hopped onto my bed as I pulled my phone out of my back pocket. And as I started crafting an email to start the process of breaking my lease, I got a slew of texts from Gavin. I ignored them long enough to get the email sent out. Then I flipped over to our conversation.

And the sheer amount of information he threw at me took me a second to digest.

**Gavin: All right, I've contacted Two Men And A Truck, and they're going to be at your place next Wednesday. They're coming with all the supplies they need to pack things up and haul things off. All you have to do is designate what you want to keep and what you**

want to throw away. What you can't bring here, they'll store in their storage facility, which will only cost about a hundred a month. Very reasonable. You can take care of it, or I can. Your choice.

**Gavin:** Also, make sure you pack a suitcase for this weekend. Be prepared for fun in the sun and lots of swimming.

**Gavin:** Oh! I almost forgot. When you come over tomorrow, choose where you want to stay. Any room is open to you as well as the guesthouse, and wherever you want to set up camp is fine with me.

**Gavin:** Did my messages go through? That was kind of a word vomit moment.

I blinked as my brain tried to register all of the information, even though it was well past midnight. But then, my fingers started typing back.

**Me:** Fun in the sun? Swimming? What are we doing this weekend?

I felt my eyes drooping as he messaged me back.

**Gavin:** It's a surprise. Just pack how you would for the beach or something and have it ready. That's all I ask. Now, I need sleep, and so do you. Get some rest, and I'll see you around... eight? Does that sound okay?

I rolled over onto my side as I wrote back.

**Me:** Perfect. I'll see you then. Night, Gavin.

**Gavin:** Night, Eva. Sleep well.

**Me:** You, too. Sweet dreams.

**Gavin:** You, too.

And as my eyes fell closed with my phone still in my hand, only one emotion registered as it filled me from head to toe.

Happiness.

I'd never felt this happy in my entire life, and I couldn't wait to start this new journey I had found for myself.

## 15

**Gavin**

"It's the day of, and you're still not going to tell us where we're going?" Eva asked.

Asia giggled. "I know where we're going."

Eva thumbed over her shoulder. "She knows, too?"

Gavin chuckled. "She thinks she knows. But she really doesn't."

Asia held her fists up in the air. "We're going to the moon!"

Eva blinked. "Okay, so she doesn't know. But, come on, Gavin. We've waited all week!"

I barked with laughter. "And you can wait another ten minutes."

This week had gone swimmingly with Eva. She was still

coming back and forth to the house, but the plans to move her in next week were solidified with the moving company. To my shock, Eva chose to stay in the main house with us instead of taking the guesthouse for herself. But, in some ways, I thought that was better. Asia would have her close at night, and it wouldn't take much for me to see her after a long day if I wanted to poke my head in and take a peek at her luscious body after a long, hard day.

And with my place slowly filling up with Eva's things and her scent, it damn near drove me wild to open that door after long days on set.

Asia gasped. "It's Trey! That's Trey!"

Eva leaned forward. "Is that... a dock?"

I nodded. "For yachts."

She eyed me closely. "Do you have a yacht, Mr. Lincoln?"

I snickered. "I've got better things to spend my time on than a yacht I'd only use every once in a while. No, no. These yachts belong to a good friend of mine, Trey. He actually flips them, you know. Like some people flip houses?"

"He flips them and then rents them out? That's actually pretty genius, especially since we're so close to the water."

I nodded. "And he had a last-minute cancellation on one of his boats."

She gawked. "Wait, we're actually going out on one of those?"

I grinned. "For the entire weekend."

My daughter cheered from the backseat. "Yay! Yay! Yay!

I'm gonna go swimming all day, Daddy. It's gonna be awesome."

I craned my neck around as I eased into a parking space. "You're darn right; it's going to be awesome. And there will be plenty of food and freshly squeezed apple juice just for you."

She kicked her legs around in excitement. "*Yay*! I love you so much, Daddy!"

I chuckled. "I love you, too, princess."

"What about drinks for the adults?" Eva asked.

My eyes found hers. "Trust me; there will be plenty of drinks and fun to be had by all people of all ages."

Trey knocked his knuckles against my window. "You gonna get out and give me a hug, man? Or, do I have to rip this door off its hinges?"

I opened my car door with a smile on my face. "Get over here, asshole."

My daughter gasped in the backseat. "That's a dirty word, Daddy!"

I clapped Trey's back as Eva wrangled my daughter out of the backseat. I held my arm out as they walked over, and I quickly introduced Eva to Trey, another good friend of mine. They shook hands before Trey tossed me a look that said, "we'll definitely be talking about this," but I shrugged it off to be dealt with later because we had weekend plans to keep.

"So, which one is ours for the weekend?" Eva asked.

Trey grinned. "I'm glad you asked. Right behind me with the beautiful red and blue decorative accents is—"

"A nightmare, that's what it is."

I furrowed my brow. "Huh?"

I watched as a shorter, stockier woman scurried up to us in a pencil skirt with her blouse tucked in. She had a couple of pencils stashed in her hair that had been twisted and pinned against her head. Her heels looked damn near deadly, and the way her face was flushed told me they'd been out here for much longer than necessary.

And when Trey cleared his throat, the short woman started talking again. "They haven't gotten anything right. We're having to change out all of the food and drinks. They fulfilled the prior order. We need at least another hour."

Trey shook his head. "We don't have another hour, Leslie. Our customers are here."

She looked at me briefly from beyond the thick, green rims of her glasses. "Right. Anyway. My point is, unless they want to eat like a vegetarian party of seven, they're going to have to wait."

Asia slid her hand into mine. "What about my juice?"

The woman peeked down at my daughter. "They actually got the apple juice right, so don't you worry about that."

"Phew," my daughter said, "that was a close one."

Eva giggled as she rubbed my back. "I don't think waiting another hour is a bad thing, do you?"

Trey chuckled. "The two of you can take the hour to get your stuff settled on the boat while we're switching out food and things of that nature. If you'll follow—"

Leslie interrupted him again. "Actually, that isn't a good idea. I've got all hands on deck; so many men are rushing on and off the boat right now to get it ready. I don't want them getting trampled."

Trey smiled down at her. "I'll take them down into the cabins and such where they can set up their rooms. It won't be an issue."

Leslie scoffed. "Trey, I'm telling you, it's not a good idea. You said so yourself that customers shouldn't see the boats until—"

Trey cut her off. "He's not just any customer. He's a good friend who has invested in my efforts, and you'll do as I tell you. Otherwise, I'll need a new assistant. Understood?"

Leslie glared up at him. "Come with me, everyone. I'll show you to your rooms."

Trey smiled and patted my shoulder, and I simply shook my head. He seemed to have his hands full with that one, but it didn't take a genius to know why he kept her around. While shorter and stockier women weren't my thing, she was definitely Trey's type. He was probably trying to get laid before he fired her or some shit. And who was I to stand in the way of my friend's happiness?

"Be careful with that one," I murmured.

Trey leaned into my ear. "I could tell you the same thing with yours."

The two of us bumped fists before Trey walked us over to the yacht. And dammit, even my own eyes almost bulged out of my head. The damn thing was a behemoth of a vessel. It could have easily been one of those yachts everyone saw in photographs that people rented to throw parties on for days on end. The red and blue accents contrasted the crisp white design, and the bright colors would be seen even from a plane flying from above, which I guess was the point if we were going to be in open waters.

"We're spending the entire weekend on this thing?" Eva asked.

Trey led us onto the yacht as people rushed and bustled around us. I heard Leslie barking orders off in the distance as Trey's smile grew. I shook my head at him before I walked over to Eva, pressing my hand against the small of her back.

And when she looked up at me, I winked. "All weekend. I already have the perfect place for us to dock as well. There's this small, sandy island about ten miles off the coast. We can dock there, sleep on the yacht, and then jump off the edge of the boat and swim right from a private little beach where we can sunbathe, hang out, and just be together."

Her jaw hit the floor as her eyes danced around the massive boat. Yet again, I got a chance to shock her to her very core, and I loved it. I had stunned her into silence as she pulled away from me, allowing her fingertips to run across the smooth, wooden railing that ran along the expanse of the outer rim of the yacht.

And Asia was so excited that she rushed down the steps to claim her room with her bag in her hand.

"I'll show her to her room, you guys!" Leslie called up.

Trey yelled down the stairs at her. "She's in the room farther to the back!"

"Yeah! I know! I've worked with you for five years, remember?"

I chuckled. "She's a spitfire."

Trey sighed. "And she keeps me in line, which is exactly what I need."

I stood beside my friend. "So, what can we expect from this weekend? Because I'm not going to lie, I didn't realize we'd be booking out the biggest yacht in the damn marina. Especially with the little you charged me for this stuff."

He shrugged. "We're using as much as we can from what we've already ordered for the party that canceled because you know how I hate waste. So, there wasn't much else to purchase. They had to forfeit their deposit, so that chiseled away half of what I would've charged you upfront in the first place."

"I really appreciate it, man. Seriously."

He smiled at me. "Just make lots of memories. Good ones. Okay?"

"You got yourself a deal there, man. Thanks for this."

He clapped my back with a tight hug one last time before we started following behind Eva as she walked around to take everything in.

"There will be a small staff of two working for you during the weekend. Their cabin entrances are separate from yours, so you won't see them often. One will be cooking fresh foods and snacks, and the other is your bartender. They'll be on the clock from sunup to sundown unless you release them earlier."

I nodded. "Anything else I need to know?"

Trey shrugged. "Just treat her with care. Don't dock her on the sand. Shit like that."

"I'll take good care of her. I promise."

"I know you will. It's the only reason why I considered doing this for you. You're always good to my stuff, so I'm not worried. Leslie!"

I heard her heels clicking behind us. "What?"

He turned around. "Is everything ready?"

I peered over my shoulder and sat Leslie nodding her head as she ticked off a checklist. "There's one more box I need to track down, and then we'll be good."

Trey smiled at me. "Perfect. We'll get out of your hair, then, and the three of you can set sail in about ten minutes."

I felt my phone vibrate in my pocket. "Again, I really appreciate this. Thank you."

"You three enjoy yourselves, and we'll see you around noon on Sunday."

I pulled my phone out of my pocket. "See you then, man."

Trey and Leslie walked off while they softly bickered about something, and my stomach hit the floor. Of course, I had a text message from Marissa. It was like every time my life started on a good path, she felt it in the ethers and just had to spoil the moment. I peeked around and saw Eva with my daughter as they gazed out toward the ocean, pointing at the fish swimming around the bow of the boat.

So, I slinked off into the lower cabins and tucked myself away to read this damn message.

**Marissa: Just wanted to let you know that I snagged another modeling gig in Paris. Kind of like the one I did a couple of years ago, but I'll be gone longer this time. We need to talk.**

I felt my entire body tense as I typed a message back.

**Gavin: How long will you be gone this time?**

Those three little dots danced around for a while. In fact, almost three entire minutes passed by before only two words popped up on the screen. Two little words that made me see red.

**Marissa: Six months.**

My hands started trembling as she quickly sent another message on the heels of that one.

**Marissa: I thought we could have this conversation on the phone, but I guess I can ask here. I'd like you and Asia to come with me to Paris for those six months. I think she'd love it since she loves traveling, and you could take a break like you always talk about doing.**

I decided to call her because I sure as hell wasn't typing out this conversation with her. And the phone didn't even get through the first ring before she picked up.

"Is this a good call or a bad one?" she asked.

I drew in a sobering breath, trying to calm my raging anger. "Since when did you think I wanted a break from my career?"

"You talked about it all the time when we were married."

"Yeah, and then we got divorced, and I realized it was you I needed the break from."

She scoffed. "Well, ouch."

I pinched the bridge of my nose. "Asia and I aren't going to Paris with you. No way."

"Did you even ask her what she thought about it?"

"She's seven. She doesn't have enough forethought to understand what I'd be asking her. And besides, what would she do about school?"

"I mean, you'd be taking time off work, so you could homeschool her."

I blinked. "So, I leave behind my career that I've worked so hard for to homeschool our daughter halfway across the world while you pose for pictures for six months."

She sighed. "Why the hell do you always have to belittle what I do for a living?"

"I'm not belittling your job; I'm belittling your critical thinking skills."

"You know what? I've had enough of this conversation already. All I needed was a yes or a no. That's it."

"Well, the answer is no."

"And there's not even room for discussion?"

I leaned against the wall. "You didn't say that. You just said yes or no."

Her voice grew harsh. "Since when did you start being such an asshole?"

"Since you started assuming that you could go out and prioritize yourself while still dropping in whenever you wanted to in order to play Mom. Do you know how much you've turned my life upside down because you can't do what's best for Asia? Do you know how much I've had to sift through and how much I've had to plan just to get regular help for her so you can go gallivanting off and play the card of 'single working mother' while I'm back here actually being a parent?"

She hissed at me. "Well, I also take these jobs because I'm more than just a mother. My career is just as important as yours."

I scoffed. "Yeah, and if you really wanted to co-parent, we should have talked about this before you even took the damn contract in the first place. But, you didn't think about that, did you? You just thought you could call, make demands, and talk me into changing my mind when you knew the answer would be 'no.' So, why are you wasting my time?"

"I'm sorry, I'm not sure who's on the phone, but if you could put my Gavin back on, that'd be great."

I growled at her. "I haven't been yours in a while, and I never will be again. We co-parent, but that's it. Understood?"

"You really are a piece of work, you absolute shithead. I'm done talking about this. I shouldn't even have to discuss my career moves with you when you don't even do that with me."

I felt my voice rising. "I always talk about my career when it takes me out of the damn country, Marissa! I've talked with you about it every single time! And every single time it comes up, you come up with a damn good reason why I shouldn't go, so I don't. Do you know how much that has stunted my career? But, I willingly do it to keep the peace between us and to try to provide some sort of stability for Asia. Do you not care about any of that?"

There was silence on her end for a long time. But, when she spoke, her words were sound and calm, which told me just how angry I had made her.

"If you can yell at me like that, then you're obviously yelling at our daughter like that, and I won't stand for it."

Disbelief filled my veins. "And what I won't stand for is my daughter having a selfish mother who calls her an accident right in front of her, dumps her into my lap when it's convenient for her, then goes around lying to me about small things like firing some nanny I hired that actually had to quit because she got pregnant."

She shrieked at me. "And we wouldn't even be having this argument right now if you weren't absolutely insistent on the fact that I keep our child in the first place!"

Her words spun my head, and I lost control of my mouth. "Well, then I guess you'll be hearing from my lawyer when I file for sole custody. So, be on the lookout for that paperwork."

"Gavin, wait. I'm—"

I hung up the phone on her and pinched the bridge of my nose. I drew in deep, sobering breaths, trying to calm myself down from my raging high. My hands quaked. My knees felt weak. The world spun around me, threatening to make me sick. But, above my head, I heard the pitter-patter of feet before my daughter's and Eva's giggles flooded down the stairs to my left.

I decided to put a pin in my issues and go be with the only two people important to me right now. After all, we had a date with the open waters to keep.

## 16

**Eva**

I stood behind Asia while Gavin commanded the wheel up at the top of the yacht. As we eased away from the shoreline, with the entirety of the ocean stretched out before us, I knew I'd never experience anything more powerful or more peaceful than being in that moment. The ocean breeze kicked up, wafting my hair behind my shoulders as Asia leaned against me. And with her head tucked just below my bosom, her tiny little hands settled on top of mine.

As we watched, the island came into view.

"I see it! I see it! Look!" she exclaimed.

I smiled. "I see it, too. Our own little island, just for us."

"Daddy!" she shrieked.

"I'm pulling closer, princess!" Gavin yelled down.

I stroked my fingers through her delicate, soft tendrils as the ocean parted for us. Waves sloshed against the boat as we pulled up to the island, stopping less than thirty feet away from the shoreline. Asia and I peered over the edge, taking in the clearer waters. We watched all of the little rainbow-colored fish swim beneath the surface. And as Gavin dropped the anchor, I breathed in the salted scent of calm and peace, a feeling that surrounded me as the boat finally stilled.

"So," Gavin said as he leaped down the stairs, "who's up for a bonfire and roasting marshmallows."

Asia's eyes bulged, and she pulled away from me. "I am, Daddy! I am! Can we do it now? *Please?*"

I turned. "Yeah, Daddy. Can we do it now?"

The second the sentence flew out of my mouth, Gavin's eyes whipped over to mine. And the darkness that shrouded his gaze stopped my heart in my chest. His gaze wafted down my body, drinking me in as he held his daughter close.

But, when his stare found my gaze once more, I knew I was in for a hell of a night.

A hell of a beautiful night.

"Of course, we can do it now. But, we have to swim to shore. Think you can swim that far?" Gavin asked.

Asia jumped with joy. "Yes, I can! I've been practicing. I'm gonna go put on my floaties and bathing suit. I'll be right back!"

And with that, she dashed off, leaving Gavin and me alone on the deck as he slowly sauntered toward me. His shadow swallowed me whole, and then he had my back pinned against the railing of the boat.

"Daddy, huh?" he asked.

I blinked. "It just—kind of came rushing out."

His lips dipped down to my ear. "Plenty more will come rushing out tonight if you play your cards right."

The bones evaporated from my knees. "I look forward to it, then."

His eyes came back to mine one last time before he backed up, leaving me panting softly and wanting more of him. He winked at me then turned his back, making his way for the stairs so he could get changed. And after he came back up in nothing but his bathing suit, I had to keep myself from staring at the solid lines disappearing beyond the waist of his pants—lines that led to something I wanted to taste between my lips.

*Keep it together. You two aren't alone this weekend.*

The voice in my head spoke of reason, but my thighs spoke of something much more salacious. Still, I managed to get into my two-piece bathing suit before I slathered on a bit of sunscreen. I couldn't be too careful with my complexion, and by the time I made my way back up to the front of the yacht, I heard splashing in the water.

I peered over the edge to see Gavin and Asia already swimming to shore, with Asia splashing him every chance she got.

So, I dove in and headed after them.

Feeling the water rushing over my body cleansed me in a

way I didn't realize I had needed. Pulling myself through the oceanic expanse before I came up for air made me feel alive. Rejuvenated. As if I were getting a fresh start on my life. I swam my way to shore, riding on the backs of the rolling waves that eventually tumbled me onto the sand.

And when Gavin took my hand, he pulled me up to my feet with ease. "Come on. I pulled the cooler behind me, so we've got drinks and snacks along with marshmallows."

I almost got lost in his mesmerizing stare. "I'll go find sticks for us to put the marshmallows on."

He grinned. "Guess I'll start gathering firewood. Asia?"

She called out to him. "Yeah, Daddy?"

"Don't go in beyond your knees. Eva and I have to go find stuff for the fire, okay?"

"Okay!"

I furrowed my brow with worry. "Should we take turns so someone stays with her?"

He chuckled. "Trust me, Asia won't venture out past her ankles. She doesn't like being in the water by herself. We'll probably come back to a massive sandcastle. Plus, the tree line is riddled with downed trees. I don't think we'll have to venture that far to get what we need."

With a nod of my head, we were off. And thirty minutes later, we had a fire going, and our first round of marshmallows were divvied out. The sun had barely begun to set as we roasted up our dessert first. And after the marshmallows were depleted, Gavin pulled out hot dogs and buns from the cooler.

Hot dogs we roasted on sticks and the buns were crisped up at the corner of the fire pit.

We ate until we could hardly move, then we started the slow journey back to the boat. Colors splashed across the sky, drawing in the nighttime as the moon soared above our heads in a foggy, almost reflective outline. Gavin helped us both back onto the boat since we were all stuffed to the brim, and after we got changed out of our wet clothes, it was time to tuck Asia in.

I swear, she was asleep before I even pressed a kiss to the top of her head.

But, once I got back to the bow of the ship where Gavin stood, he turned around and handed me a very colorful drink.

"For you, courtesy of our bartender," he said.

I smiled. "Thank you. This looks delicious."

"I went ahead and dismissed them for the night since I figured we wouldn't be hungry after everything we ate."

"Well, what about drinks? I might want another one of these."

He wrapped his arm around my waist. "Which is why I had the bartender set out everything I'd need to make you as many as you want."

"My hero," I sighed playfully.

But, he only pulled me closer. "Maybe one day, you'll let me be just that."

Gavin swayed my body side to side softly as we gazed into each other's eyes. We sipped on our drinks as we slowly twirled around, our bodies ushering in the heavy night sky.

Stars twinkled by the millions just above our heads. The water stretched out as far as our eyes could see, and the world was dead silent. I finished my drink and set it on a random table. Gavin danced us next to where he set his empty glass down as well.

Then, he took my hand in his, and away we went, dancing from one end of the ship to the other.

I had no words for how romantic it all felt. I had no comments to rebut the flagrant admission Gavin had just given me. He wanted to be my hero? What did that even mean? Did it mean he wanted to be my everything? That he wanted to save me from a life less lived?

Either way, I felt myself melting against him as I laid my head against his chest. The moonlight played wonderfully off his eyes, and I knew that if I gazed into them any longer, they'd suck me in and I'd never want to return.

But, it seemed as if we had similar thoughts because out of nowhere, we stopped dancing. Out of nowhere, I felt his finger crook beneath my chin. And out of nowhere, he dragged my gaze to meet his before he uttered the words I'd been longing to hear from him since the first day I'd met him.

"You're the most beautiful woman I've ever seen, Eva. I want you to know that."

I drew in a sharp breath to tell him that I felt the same way. About him, that was. I'd been wanting to tell him for a while now exactly how sexy he was to me. I wanted to proclaim how much I enjoyed our time together. How much I appreciated him making me feel the way he did. But, before I could part my lips to utter even one word, his mouth crashed against mine.

His tongue parted my lips.

His arms cloaked my back, pulling me closer as my knees gave way.

And as we sank to the floor of the deck of the ship, I decided to lose myself in him. To accept whatever came my way, no matter the possible heartache attached. Gavin would always be worth it, even if we ended up only being a temporary thing.

## 17

**Gavin**

She was too much for me. Her presence was too much for me. And watching her parade around in that little bikini she had on earlier kept me at a constant state of attention all fucking day. Watching the stars swirl in her eyes kicked up a feeling within me that I'd never felt toward another woman before. Having her in my arms made me feel more powerful and stronger than I'd ever felt in my entire life. And when her legs parted to accommodate me, it felt like coming home.

Eva felt like home to me, and I never wanted it to end.

"Gavin, oh fuck," she panted.

I kissed down her neck, allowing my tongue to explore her. I pulled her bikini top down with my teeth, feeling her naked breasts pop out against my face. I nuzzled against them. I lapped at her puckered peaks until they were tightened mounds against her creamy skin. Her hands running through my hair sent me onward toward my goal while my mouth salivated for the meal to come.

And after sliding her legs over my shoulders, I pulled her bikini bottoms off to the side before parting her folds with my tongue.

"Shit," she hissed.

Her nails raked softly against my scalp, and it only spurred me onward. I shoved my bathing suit down my legs until I kicked it off with my feet, my body bared to a watery world around us. I lapped at her swollen clit, feeling her buck against me as I undid all of the bows that kept her bikini against her body. I wanted to see the moonlight illuminate her curves. I wanted to feel all of her against me as my body proclaimed my love for her.

I loved this fucking woman.

And I'd be damned if I let her go without a fight.

"Gavin, I need to feel you. Please."

I sucked her clit between my teeth and growled. "I want to feel you come for me."

Her hands ripped me up by my hair, tugging me all the way up her body. She crashed our lips together, licking her juices off my skin before her eyes met mine. Her pupils were blown wide open, swallowing her gorgeous stare and leaving nothing but a pleasure-hungry monster for me to devour.

And fucking hell, I'd never seen anything sexier than that.

"Now," she demanded.

I grinned. "As you wish, beautiful."

I lined my cock up and shoved myself inside of her, not once letting her catch her breath. Her eyes bulged, and her back arched as she choked out her sounds while my hips pounded against her. I folded her body in half. I tossed her legs over my shoulders and held her down until she was helpless beneath me. My cock was drenched with her arousal. My balls filled with her heat. My skin, seated against hers as her juices splashed against my abs.

With every thrust, I fell deeper into her.

With every roll of my hips, my tight curls caressed her clit.

And as her hands raked up and down my arms, I felt her body quivering for me. Quaking for me. Aching for release as I lost myself in the way she smelled and looked and sounded.

"Holy fuck, I'm so close," I growled.

She whimpered with a need for release. "Please, please, please, please. Gavin, I can't—it's all—oh, shit."

I felt her pussy clamp down around me, sending me spiraling into the open waters of my mind. I collapsed against her, my muscles contracting and releasing as my cock filled her to the brim. She milked my dick, taking everything she could before her body relaxed against the deck of the boat.

And as I pressed lazy kisses against her shoulder, I let my dick stay sheathed inside of her.

I wasn't ready to give up the feeling of home just yet.

"The stars are beautiful," she whispered.

I groaned as I rolled over, taking her with me as her head fell against my chest. Her leg slipped between mine as I wrapped my arms around her, holding her closely at my side. And she was right; the millions of stars twinkling above our heads clapped for our performance amidst a pitch-black sky.

I'd never seen anything like it in all my life. "Wow," I murmured, "you weren't kidding."

"I don't know about you, but I'm ready for a drink. You want something?"

I kissed her forehead. "I'd love something. Want me to make it?"

She stood to her feet, even though she looked wobbly. "I've got it. You lay there and rest. You do so much for me, so let me do something for you."

I let my eyes linger on her nakedness. "Fine by me."

She flushed a deep shade of pink that made me love her even more as she quickly made her way over to the bar. She started pulling things out and stared at them blankly before settling on Jack and Coke for us to sip. I smiled as she brought it to me. I pressed myself up as she headed for the two lounge chairs at the back of the ship that gazed out over the watery horizon. Small waves whitecapped and died down as I rummaged around for a blanket to throw over our naked bodies.

And after we settled on the lounge chairs, I placed my hand on Eva's bare thigh while we sipped our drinks.

"Want to talk about it?" she asked.

I peered over at her. "About what?"

"Whatever it is that's on your mind."

I snickered as I gazed back out toward the water. "That easy to read, huh?"

She placed her hand on top of mine beneath the blanket and squeezed. "Maybe just a tad."

I chuckled mindlessly. "I suppose I can if you want me to."

"I won't make you do anything you don't want to do. But, I'm here if you want someone to listen."

And her sentiment was enough to get my lips moving. "I had a conversation with Marissa before we set sail."

"Your ex-wife, right?"

I looked over at her and nodded. "Right."

"I take it the conversation didn't go well?"

My eyes found the water again as I threw back the rest of my drink. "Not in the slightest."

"What happened? I mean, what did you two talk about?"

*She should stay up to date with everything that affects Asia. She's her nanny, after all.*

I cleared my throat. "Marissa called to tell me that she'd taken a job in Paris that would take her away for six months."

"Oh. That doesn't sound too bad, especially now that I'm helping out. Right?"

My gaze gravitated slowly back to her. "She asked Asia and me to come with her."

She clicked her tongue. "Ah. That would be the hang-up."

I chuckled. "It's not the only hang-up. Marissa's done

many things I don't agree with. For starters, she can apparently take any overseas contract she wants, but I have to tell her whenever I'm offered that kind of gig. And ever since our divorce, I haven't been able to take a single one of them because of the hell she raises over it. She calls it 'sticking her with her daughter without help.' I call it 'being the single parent she proclaims to be.'"

"Wow, that's very unfair."

I drew in a deep breath. "Oh, it gets better. The last time Asia was in the hospital because of her asthma, my ex blurted out the fact that our daughter was an 'accident.'"

"What? Don't tell me she heard."

And when I didn't respond, Eva's face grew red with anger. "I can't believe she said something like that. Maybe you didn't plan her, sure. But Asia is no fucking accident, Gavin."

It warmed my heart to hear how much it angered Eva because it showed me how much she already cared about my little girl. "I know. And then on the phone, when I threw that in her face—which I probably shouldn't have done, but I can't take it back now—she said that if I hadn't forced her to have Asia, we wouldn't even be having the argument we were having in the first place."

Her jaw dropped open. "I'm sorry, but did you marry Satan?"

I barked with laughter and turned my attention back out to the water. "Some days, I feel like I did. And my head popped off so quickly that I told her the next time she heard from me, it would be through my lawyer after I submitted paperwork to get sole custody of Asia."

"I think that's a fantastic idea."

My head whipped back over to her. "You do?"

She nodded. "I do. If that's really the kind of atmosphere Asia's around with her mother, and if her mother really says shit like that in front of her, then it's what you have to do. Asia doesn't deserve that, and it sounds like Marissa doesn't even want to be a parent. She just wants all of the accolades that come with being one."

"Thank you! Finally, someone that gets it."

She squeezed my hand. "Either way, I support you one hundred percent."

And with those words, I felt myself fall just a little bit more in love with this wonderful woman who had come soaring into my life. I only hoped that I didn't find a way to fuck it up for good.

Eva yawned. "Well, I don't know about you, but I'm ready for some sleep."

I stood to my feet. "Want to wake up with me in the morning and watch the sunrise? We could have breakfast together before Asia gets up."

She stood and giggled. "I'd love nothing more. But I'll need help finding my room. I wasn't sure which one I was supposed to be in, so I got changed in your room instead."

"Why can't you just sleep in there with me, then? It's got a king-sized bed."

"Asia won't think that's weird?"

I shrugged. "We'll be up before her anyway for the sunrise, right?"

Her smile grew bigger. "Lead the way, then, handsome."

And not another word was needed before I scooped her into my arms, walked her into my room, and tumbled into bed with her, ready to hold her in my arms all night long.

## 18

**Eva**

I drew in a deep breath and yawned as my eyes naturally fell open. The high thread-count sheets felt amazing against my sun-warmed skin. I stretched my arms over my head, feeling the sheet fall down just past my breasts. But, when my arms dropped, I heard someone grunt beside me, and a soft giggle sounded outside the door.

"Wake up, Daddy! We gotta do more swimming!"

I clapped my hand over my mouth, and Gavin bolted upright in his bed. He scrambled for his phone and groaned, realizing we had not only missed the sunrise but probably breakfast as well.

"Shit," he hissed.

I pulled the sheet over my head while he got dressed. And

when I heard him slip out the door, I slowly peeked out from beyond the covers. I heard Gavin coaxing Asia up the steps with promises of morning ice cream cones and sweet treats, buying me just enough time to leap out of bed and throw on clothes.

Then, with my head held high and my wits about me, I started out of the room and up toward the table near the kitchen on the yacht's main level, where Asia was already eating her fill of Neapolitan ice cream with whipped cream on top.

"Figured I'd bribe her," Gavin said with a chuckle.

"Hi," Asia said with her mouth full.

I decided to sit beside the little girl, figuring it was the safest option for now. "Leave some for the rest of us; I was hoping to have a bowl of ice cream myself."

Asia giggled. "There are three whole gallons. You can have your own, okay?"

My eyebrows rose. "Sounds like a plan to me. You can just sit the carton in front of me, and I can dig a spoon into it."

Asia laughed with delight. "No, you can't, silly! Gotta use a bowl, like this."

She made a show of lifting her bowl before she dipped her spoon into it and scooped up a massive bite of chocolate and vanilla ice cream. She got it all over her face, trying to get it into her little mouth, and the sight made me giggle. The chef hired to be with us for the weekend set a mug of coffee in front of me before placing a little tray down with creamer and sugar on it. Then, two massive plates of food were set in front of me.

One was filled with fruits of all shapes, colors, and sizes. And the other one was loaded with eggs, bacon, hash browns, and pancakes.

"Whoa," Asia said.

I snickered. "Whoa, is right."

Gavin unfolded the napkin around his silverware. "Now, *this* is what I call breakfast."

Asia lowered her voice to a whisper. "Eva?"

I mocked her tone of voice. "Yes?"

"Are you gonna eat all that?"

I giggled and shook my head, still whispering. "Not at all. You wanna share?"

She scooted her bowl to me. "Share for a share?"

I dipped my spoon into her ice cream. "I love that idea. Thank you."

"Thank you, too."

The three of us passed our plates and bowls, sampling each other's food and humming over how gloriously fresh it tasted. The sun rose slowly in the sky, beating down against us while the rushing ocean wind kept the napes of our necks cool. Waves sloshed against the boat as it softly rocked side to side. Asia scooted her chair close to me and tossed her legs into my lap as she polished off her great, big bowl of ice cream.

I was getting much too attached to the cute, button-nosed little girl, and I knew that spelled trouble for me in the long run, especially if I screwed things up with Gavin.

*I need to talk to Margo and Ginger.*

But, they wouldn't be accessible until after we got back to the city.

I needed reassurance that what I was feeling wasn't wrong. And if it was wrong, I needed my two best friends' advice to help me navigate these treacherous high seas. Things didn't feel wrong between myself and Gavin, even though it felt weird to be fucking around with the man who had just hired me to be his nanny.

Did that make things wrong between us completely? Or were my insecurities getting in the way?

*I really should've told the girls about this when we were on the phone last time.*

I mean, things couldn't go on like this, right? Things couldn't just be happily ever after, then end. Right?

"Eva?"

Asia's voice pulled me from my day dreams. "Yes, honey?"

"You wanna have a sleepover when we get home?"

I smiled. "I'd love to have a sleepover. Wanna sleep in your bed or mine?"

"We can do mine. I have a canopy, so we can sleep like princesses."

"Oh, I like that idea a lot. Do princesses get snacks?"

Gavin cleared his throat. "Not in bed, they don't."

Asia giggled. "But we can have snacks *before* bed. That's good, too."

"What if we had the sleepover in my bed and had snacks there? Surely, Daddy doesn't control what happens in my room."

I felt Gavin's eyes on me. "Wanna bet?"

My eyes met his. "Sure. What's the wager?"

I tried to keep my smile buried, but when he smiled at me, I couldn't take it. The damn thing spread across my face like wildfire, and soon we were all laughing and talking about these massive sleepover plans that snowballed out of control. We went from sleeping in my bed and having snacks to sleeping in the guesthouse, having seven different friends, and staying up all night to eat twelve different kinds of sugar-laced snacks.

"I think this is a good plan," Asia said.

I tucked a strand of her hair behind her ear. "Daddy and I will talk about it, then let you know. How does that sound?"

She leaned close to me and whispered again, "Don't let him win. He always wins, but I think you can take him."

I peeked over at Gavin. "Me, too."

He smirked. "Wanna bet?"

I giggled. "Sure, what's the wager again?"

I got so wrapped up in the heart-warming conversation Asia and I were having that I didn't realize Gavin had finished and gotten up from the table. It wasn't until I looked over at him to get his opinion on something that I saw he wasn't even sitting there any longer.

"Don't worry, he does that a lot," Asia said.

I nodded mindlessly. "Right. Uh, Asia?"

"Yeah?"

"Can you do me a favor?"

She yawned. "Okay."

I kissed the top of her head. "Go downstairs to your room and take your time getting changed. We're going to get in our bathing suits, let our food settle a bit, then we're going to go swimming."

Her eyes bulged. "In five minutes?"

I bopped her nose with my finger. "In thirty minutes."

"Aww, man."

I cupped her cheek. "We've got all day today and the morning tomorrow to do lots of swimming. No pouting, okay? In thirty minutes, we'll jump in. But, you need to get your swimsuit on first and let that food rest."

She jutted her bottom lip out. "I don't know how to make it rest. They don't have blankets or stuffed animals to keep them company."

I shrugged. "I suppose you could eat one."

"What?"

"Want me to get you a blanket? I hear they're tasty with ketchup."

She giggled with delight. "That's gross, Eva! You don't eat blankets."

"Well, then get into your bathing suit and get underneath the covers of your bed. Because if you're covered, then they're covered, and they can rest for a bit before we go swimming for the rest of the day. Okay?"

She leaped up from her seat. "Okay, I can do that!"

She took off toward the steps and soon disappeared below the deck. Then, I set off in search of Gavin. I walked around the outside of the yacht and didn't so much as hear his voice. So, I started downstairs to the lower level where our cabins were.

I heard Asia's soft snoring coming from her room, which I fully expected. But, what I didn't expect was to hear Gavin's voice behind a closed door.

And when I inched it open, I found him perched on the edge of his bed with his back toward the door while on what seemed to be a video call.

"When do they need me by?" he asked.

I had no idea how the hell he had any sort of service in the middle of the ocean to use for a video call, but I also didn't question it. However, I couldn't stop myself from eavesdropping.

"So, the filming is in California?" he asked.

I strained to hear the foreign voice, but I didn't catch what they were saying.

"Two weeks? Just to interview? What kind of interview is it?"

I furrowed my brow and closed my eyes, trying my best to pay attention.

"Yes, I know it's a massive project," Gavin said. "But, I've got my daughter, and I need—yes, I hired a nanny, but—I get that, dammit. It's just—no, I'm sorry. I didn't mean to curse at you. It's—thank you. Yes. I agree; I am at the peak of my career."

Then finally, the voice on the other side of the conversation grew loud enough for me to hear.

"That's right, and with you being at the peak of your career comes demanding hours and even longer filming schedules. Isn't this what you wanted?"

Then, Gavin spoke the words that broke my heart. "More than anything, you know that."

The foreign voice continued, "Then, it's time to start acting like it. Two weeks in Hollywood, at the end of the month. Work it out, or I'll have to suggest someone else on my roster for the job."

"I'll work it out. Whatever it takes."

My heart sank to my feet, and I silently closed the door. Tears rushed my eyes as I backtracked toward the stairs and made my way toward the bar. I flagged down the bartender and mindlessly ordered a drink, hoping I could drown my tears in alcohol and suck it up before Gavin got back up here.

I was nothing but his daughter's caretaker. I knew that now. And I surely couldn't expect a man with a life like Gavin's to put all of that aside—his dreams and his wants and his wishes—to be with someone like myself.

And while my heart broke for the things that could never be between us, I still hoped Gavin took the interview.

If anything, so he could continue chasing his dreams like he should have been in the first place.

## 19

**Gavin**

"I'm serious; I'll make it work. I'll be there for the interview," I said.

My agent nodded. "Wonderful, I'll let them know. And I'll send you confirmation of your plane tickets as soon as I have them."

"All right. Gotta go, but we'll talk soon."

He pointed at me. "I want to hear from you the second you're on land. Don't go dying on me or anything."

I resisted the urge to roll my eyes. "Trust me. You'll get your paycheck. I promise."

I hung up the video call without giving him a chance to rebut. I hated the way he talked with me sometimes, but he always had a point. And more often than not, he was right. I had taken a serious hiatus from my career because of this bullshit. If I stayed away much longer, I wouldn't be nearly as relevant.

As my agent always barked at me, if I wasn't willing to put in the work, someone else behind me was.

But, I still wanted to focus on the rest of the weekend. So, I quickly got changed into my bathing suit and headed up the stairs. I looked around for Eva and my daughter, wondering where the hell they had gotten off to. However, when I heard giggling and splashing around, all I had to do was look over the edge of the boat.

"Hey there!" I called out.

Asia looked up at me and waved. "Look, Daddy! Eva and I are playing dunks. Watch!"

She lunged at Eva, and the woman playfully screamed before she went under the water. Asia giggled with delight and swam around, flailing her arms dramatically as she shouted, "I win again!" The sight warmed my heart, but it also hung a question heavily in my mind.

Could I really jet off to Hollywood and leave my daughter in round-the-clock care with her? I mean, it was one thing to be gone daily. But, it was another thing not to step foot back into the house for two damn weeks. Did I trust Eva enough to take care of my daughter like that? There was so much I had to prepare if that was really the case. I had to call the doctors and get her on Asia's HIPAA forms. I had to contact Asia's school and let them know that someone else would be picking her up and dropping her off for a while because she'd start before I'd get back home from this damned thing.

Then, a thought occurred to me.

Most of my projects were in Hollywood. Most of my friends were in Hollywood. Hell, my fucking agent was in Hollywood, yet I lived in Florida, of all places. So, what if I moved? It wasn't completely unheard of, and there were tons of homes always popping up on the market around that area. I could buy a house outright, pay the property taxes upfront for a few years, and ensure Asia a stable environment for the next five or so years until I got my career back up and running.

But, could I really uproot her away from all of this?

To Asia, Key Biscayne was home. All of her friends were here. Her mother still lived in this area, despite the issues we were currently having. And if I moved to Hollywood, what about Eva? Would she come with us and keep helping?

Could I really uproot both of them for something selfish like my career?

Water splashed against my face before my daughter started laughing. It pulled me out of my trance long enough to hear her yell, "Jump in, Daddy!" So, I did. I let myself forget about my worries for a split second, and I stood on the ledge of the boat before jumping in. I curled my knees up to my chest, listened as my daughter shrieked with joy, and then the cool water of the ocean wrapped around me as I tore into the crystal-clear waves that sloshed against our own little private island.

And when I came back up for air, I found Eva swimming toward me.

"You have to come to see what I found. Asia!"

My daughter turned around. "Yeah?"

"Come see what I found! Hurry!"

We all swam for the shoreline, and I saw what Eva was talking about. There were hundreds of little holes that had popped up everywhere, and every time the waves lapped against the shoreline, these little, tiny crabs popped their heads out in order to enjoy it. Asia giggled and clapped her hands as she bent down and looked into the teeny, tiny little holes. Eva leaned against me, her fingers playing with mine as I stole a soft kiss against the top of her head while no one was looking. And I watched my daughter dig around in the sand for the little crabs, committing the sight to memory. Because I knew in the blink of an eye, she'd be a teenager and want nothing to do with me.

"This was a great catch," I said.

Eva giggled. "I knew she'd like them. The waves carried me to shore, and I stepped on one. That's how I found them."

I peered down at her. "You okay? Do I need to take a look at your foot?"

She giggled and looked up into my eyes. "They're so tiny that it felt like I stepped on a sharp edge more than anything. It didn't even break the skin."

I took her hand within mine. "As long as you're all right."

She kissed the back of my hand. "I'll always be all right when I'm with you."

Her words soared my heart into the heavens, but it gave me even more to think about. We spent the day swimming and splashing around with one another, and when our stomachs started growling around four in the afternoon, we swam back to the yacht. We climbed up and smelled the chef already preparing dinner for us, so we parted ways to shower and get changed into fresh pairs of clothes.

But, once we emerged for dinner, I heard my daughter's snoring echoing down the small cabin hallway.

Eva giggled. "Poor girl wore herself out."

I placed my hand on the small of her back. "We'll save her some. I'm sure she'll be up in a couple of hours with a ravenous appetite."

"You sure we shouldn't wake her? Just in case she wants to eat with us?"

I walked her to the stairs. "For all we know, she won't be up until morning."

"But, she's only had one meal today."

I chuckled. "I promise she'll be fine. She does this from time to time. Just let her sleep."

Eva sighed as she walked up the stairs. "If you insist."

I grinned. "Trust me, I insist wholeheartedly."

As easy as things felt between us, though, our conversation at dinner was stunted. I had too much on my mind, but Eva wasn't offering up much discussion, either. I figured maybe she was tired or burnt out from her time in the sun. But, she didn't even look up at me for much of the meal.

She simply kept her head down, took bites, and only afforded me a head-nod or two whenever I said something.

"So, you have a good day?" I asked.

She nodded and sipped her wine but didn't say anything back.

"You and Asia have fun?"

Again with a nod, but no words coming forth from her lips.

"You ready to go back tomorrow?"

She shrugged before finally offering up some sounds. "It's complicated."

I snickered. "I hear that. Sometimes, I feel like I could live on that island and build myself a little hut and be perfectly happy."

Her eyes panned out toward the setting sun. "I'd need running water, though. I'm a bit spoiled that way."

I laughed softly at her statement, but she didn't laugh back. And I knew then and there that something big was on her mind. I knew how she felt, too. I had way too much to consider concerning my career and this custody-agreement issue I dropped into my lawyer's lap only yesterday.

*I wonder if she'd come to Hollywood if I footed the bill for her trip.*

Another option was for the three of us to go to Hollywood together for the two weeks. Granted, Asia would miss the first two days of school, but it wasn't as if she'd be missing an entire week or something like that. Then, I wouldn't have to worry about my daughter being alone with Eva for so long, I'd be able to keep "coming home" to them, and we'd all be able to scout out houses together—after talking about it, of course.

*It's not fair of you to ask her to uproot her life after only knowing you a couple of weeks.*

Instead of pressing more conversation with Eva, I relegated myself to dinner in silence. I'd had plenty of them while I was still married to Marissa, and I figured one wouldn't hurt us. At least, I hoped it didn't. While I wanted to poke around inside Eva's brain and figure out what had her so preoccupied, it wasn't as if I weren't in the same boat with her or anything.

Maybe we just needed a bit of comfortable silence.

*You don't want another situation like your ex-wife, either.*

When my mind wanted to back me into a corner, it sure as hell was good at it. And the voice in my head had a point. Marissa and I moved much too quickly with things between us, and that was how we had ended up in the situation we created. The last thing I wanted was for Eva and myself to travel the same path and meet the same destructive end because we didn't do shit right the first time around. I was over the broken hearts and the manipulation. I knew falling for another woman wasn't going to solve all of my problems. If anything—with what I went through with Marissa—I knew falling in love would only create yet another delicate dynamic in my life that I'd have to treat with care.

I also knew my choice of career didn't always afford me that kind of luxury.

"I should go check on Asia just to make sure she's still sleeping," Eva said.

Her voice pulled me from the recesses of my mind, and I watched her get up. I didn't try to stop her because I heard the determination in her voice twinged with a worry that matched my own. Silently, I watched as she crossed over toward the stairs, disappearing beneath the boat without another word spoken.

And at that moment, I knew I'd never find another woman as good to my daughter and myself as her. Because dammit, she was a better mother to Asia than Marissa could ever be.

## 20

**Eva**

"Yes, up the stairs and down that middle hallway, all the way at the end. Thank you."

"Yep, that goes up there, too."

"Oh, no, no! I'll take that, thank you. That's going down here in one of the closets."

"You got it! I can do that."

"This is supposed to be in storage. You can take that back out to the truck. Thank you so much."

I pointed the men hauling my stuff into Gavin's place on where things went and what needed to be taken back to the storage facility. I had so many more things than I ever imagined, and even after donating some of my junk to the local thrift stores, I still had an entire storage container filled to the brim. Granted, most of it was furniture I wanted to keep, but some of it was of value to me. Mementos from my childhood and things I kept from my teenage years that held significance to my development. Journals I scratched my emotions into and a lockbox I kept under my bed that housed my "prized possessions" as a sixteen-year-old.

And yes, I picked the guest bedroom with the best bathroom attached to it.

Not only that, but the guest bedroom I picked out for myself had its own little second-story balcony just for me to use. Gavin had two chairs and a table set out there, as well as a little coffee machine set up in the corner so I could brew whatever I wanted and enjoy it right there on my private porch. The idea seemed nice if I could stomach the idea of coffee.

But here lately, coffee seemed to turn up my nose rather than make my mouth salivate.

"No, no, no! That goes in storage as well. Guys!"

I turned around and halted all of the movers coming through the front door. "Guys, please check the colors on the tops of the boxes. The red-topped boxes go into storage; they don't come inside. Thank you."

After our weekend away on the beach, I had come to two very stark conclusions. One, there was a good chance that I wasn't a permanent thing in Gavin's life, and I was okay with that. But, two, I had also come to terms with the fact that he and I would have regular sex while I worked for him. And I was also very much okay with it.

I mean, it was nice to daydream about playing house with some big Hollywood star, but I didn't really see him that way any longer. He was just Gavin to me—a single dad who was trying to figure out his way in life and provide the best he could for his daughter. That was it. That was the lens I saw him through, and it suited him well.

Plus, I didn't need to get attached to someone who was about to broaden a career, which meant he'd never be around.

*At least it makes sense as to why he wanted me to move in.*

Why I allowed myself to think that he wanted me to move in for other reasons, I'd never know. I chalked it up to being a naïve, idiotic little girl, and it was time for me to grow up. The days of playing house were gone, and this was the real world. I was the full-time nanny to a Hollywood A-lister, and that was that.

Nothing more, nothing less.

However, with those realizations also came a very important appointment—a doctor's appointment to get on birth control. While I'd been spending way too much money on Plan B pills after our encounters, I couldn't keep doing that shit to my body chemistry. Every time I took those damned things, they made me feel worse. And if Gavin and I were going to be sleeping with one another regularly, I needed to get my ass on birth control. It was the only responsible thing to do. I needed to start treating this less like a "coming home" situation and more like a "hook-up" situation.

So, after the movers got my stuff inside and left to put the rest of my things in storage, I headed straight for my doctor's appointment.

*Thank fuck, Gavin's got the day off today.*

I hadn't seen much of him since we had gotten back from our yacht trip, and that pretty much solidified my thoughts. We had gotten over the idea of playing house together, and we were finally coming to terms with what our relationship was really going to be like. And while I didn't want to admit how much that hurt, I knew I'd get over it. I'd been through worse in my life. A little bit of heartache over a man that was never truly mine would wash away with the ebbing and flowing of life's tides soon enough. Then, I could focus all of my attention on raising Asia to be the best version of herself she could possibly be.

I pulled into the parking lot of my doctor's office and started inside. I hadn't had a check-up in a while, so I braced myself for all sorts of things. Poking and prodding. A pap-smear and a breast exam. I bounced from room to room, giving urine samples and letting them draw blood. The doctor swabbed the inside of my cheek and checked my pupil dilation before taking my blood pressure.

But, when a nurse quickly rapped her knuckles against the door, I watched them exchange folders and glances. And it had me worried.

"Something wrong?" I asked.

Dr. Lucy flipped open the folder before she smiled. "How have you been feeling lately?"

I blinked. "I feel fine. Why?"

She snapped the folder closed. "Have you been experiencing any nausea?"

I furrowed my brow. "Uh, no?"

"Any tiredness not associated with your sleeping schedule?"

"I'm a nanny. I'm always tired."

She giggled. "What about food aversions? Turning your nose up to food or drinks you like as of late?"

I paused. "Well, I'm not really a fan of coffee anymore."

She opened the folder and scribbled something down. "Anything else?"

I racked my brain for other things. "Come to think of it, I haven't been hungry lately at all."

She peered at me from beyond the rims of her glasses. "What have you eaten in the past twenty-four hours?"

I thought back on the last day or so. "Uh, peanut butter toast. I had some chocolate milk, though that's not technically food. I, uh… oh! I had a slice of pizza last night. But, I had to pick the pepperonis off. Just smelling them gave… me…"

The doctor grinned. "Heartburn?"

My eyes slowly found hers. "No."

A smile slowly crept across her face. "Yes."

I swallowed hard. "But, that's not—that's not possible."

*Am I really pregnant?*

Another knock came at the door, and Dr. Lucy opened it. And when she did, that same nurse came jogging in with a smile on her face before she thrust a baggie into my lap. And

I felt the world tilt around me as nausea rumbled my stomach.

"Congratulations, Eva! You're pregnant!"

My doctor's voice sounded so far off as the words tumbled from her lips. I picked up the baggie and opened it, gazing into the dark expanse. There was a folder filled with pamphlets and pieces of paper. There were two bottles of pills down at the bottom of the bag. There was a small booklet entitled "What To Expect Now That You Know." There was even an appointment sheet for doctors to fill out to keep me accountable for every appointment I'd need between now and the next nine months.

"I'm pregnant," I whispered.

Dr. Lucy pulled up and chair and sat in front of me. "This is so exciting." Her eyes were alight with joy, but I couldn't help but wonder how she couldn't see the dismay written all over my face. Her bright smile didn't make this a happy occasion.

My eyes slowly raised to hers as tears lined my eyes. "Can you not read a room?"

The doctor blinked. "I'm so sorry. I thought—you just, every time I see you, you're always talking about—"

I drew in a deep breath. "I've been sleeping with someone, yes. But, every time after sex, I cruise into the pharmacy, pluck that Plan B pill right off the shelf, and I down it in the store with some water before I even pay for the stuff! How am I pregnant?"

Dr. Lucy sighed. "The Plan B pill isn't one hundred

percent effective. No form of contraception is. And the longer you wait after unprotected sex to take it, the less effective it is. On the back of the box, it says to take within twelve hours for maximum protection. Did you take it within those twelve hours?"

I blinked. "I mean, not all the time. But, it even says if you take it within a twenty-four-hour window, you're good."

"Eighty-two percent good. Not one-hundred percent good."

*My God, I'm pregnant.*

Holy shit, I was carrying Gavin's child. I felt the bag slip from my hands and fall to the floor, and I watched it crumple in silence. The entire world stilled around me as my mind flooded with so many things. I had been so broken-hearted and so preoccupied with shit going on between myself and Gavin that I hadn't even stopped to consider the fact that I hadn't had my damn period yet.

"Oh my God, I'm pregnant," I whispered.

I felt Dr. Lucy's hands on my knees. "Look up at me and breathe. You have to breathe, Eva."

I shook my head. "I can't be pregnant. Not with him. H-H-He's about to—to go and—"

"Eva, listen to me. Can you hear me?"

"I can't do this. I can't be pregnant. I can't be a single mother. I can't—I have to get out of here."

I jumped to my feet, but my knees gave way. I felt my doctor catch me before she started yelling for help, but I scrambled to try to escape. I had to get out of there. I felt the walls closing in on me. My vision started tunneling as another pair of arms wrap around my waist, and tears streaked my cheeks.

"I need to get out of here!" I exclaimed.

And the next thing I knew, the entire world became nothing but darkness.

# 21

**Gavin**

The doorbell rang, and I rushed to open it. And when I saw Jorge standing on the other side, I embraced him in a massive hug.

"You sounded pretty rough on the phone. You good?" he asked.

I squeezed him one last time before letting him go. "I've got beers out for us. I really need to talk with someone."

He nodded. "Where's Asia?"

I pointed. "Upstairs, playing. She's waiting for Eva to get back from a doctor's appointment."

Jorge crooked an eyebrow. "Everything okay with her?"

I raked my hand through my hair. "Honestly? I've got no fucking clue. That's why I need to talk."

He closed the door behind him. "Lead the way, then."

We walked into my kitchen and snatched up our beers before going to sit on the couch. I heard Asia pitter-pattering above our heads, and it made me smile, but dammit, I figured Eva would've been back from her doctor's appointment by now. She told me she was just going to get a check-up, and that was two hours ago.

Then again, I gave her the day off to get moved in and everything. So, for all I knew, she was running errands.

"All right, lover-boy. Spit it out. What's going on in that head of yours?" Jorge asked.

I cracked open my beer and chugged it back, swallowing the damned thing whole. I set the empty can on the coffee table in front of us before I leaned back into the couch cushions, and I felt Jorge staring at me with wide eyes.

"Well, guess I gotta catch up," he said.

Then, he downed his entire beer before getting up to get us more. And I didn't start talking until I had another open can in my hand.

"I have a flight I have to take in a few days to Hollywood," I said.

"For a job?" Jorge asked.

I nodded slowly. "Yep. They've got a movie that'll be filmed in their studios there, but the interview and setup alone will take me away for two weeks."

"Oh, shit. That means it's a very serious role they're considering you for."

I licked my lips. "Yep. And then the project itself will take me away for... months. You know how those jobs are."

He nudged me. "Isn't this why you hired a full-time nanny in the first place?"

I took a long pull from my beer. "You'd think, huh?"

He chuckled. "What? Don't you trust her? Or, you don't want to leave her?"

I shrugged as I stared off at the wall. "Why can't it be a little bit of both?"

"You like this girl, don't you?"

"I mean, she's a good girl. She's smart. Very pretty. Absolutely wonderful with Asia. She's a good addition to the house."

"How does Marissa feel about her?"

I scoffed. "Marissa's currently preoccupied with battling my request for full custody. So, I don't think she gives a rat's ass right now."

He cocked his body to face me. "Whoa-ho-ho! Finally taking my advice there, huh? I've been telling you for years to challenge that custody agreement. That woman has no right to being the custodial parent. Not with that attitude she's got all the time."

I groaned. "Trust me, I know. A lot happened during our weekend at sea that we took, but that was the first of many wrenches thrown into my plan."

"And what's this big, grand plan of yours?"

I snickered. "Is it weird that I don't actually know?"

He patted my shoulder. "I think you do know, but you're simply afraid to say it out loud."

I slowly looked over at him. "You think?"

"I know. Gavin, you've been a completely different person ever since Eva came into the picture. You've been more...alive. You've had more pep in your step. You've smiled more in these past couple of weeks than I've seen you smile in months. Years, even."

I blinked. "It's only been a couple of weeks?"

He grinned. "Sometimes, life moves quickly. But, if you don't move with it, you might lose it. Get what I'm saying?"

I threw back the rest of my second beer. "Yeah, I think so."

He nudged me again. "So, start by admitting it. Say the words out loud. I swear you'll feel better once you do."

I shook my head. "I don't know. What if I fuck this up like I fucked it up with Marissa?"

"Hey, look at me."

I peered over at him before his hand cupped the back of my head, forcing me to pay attention. "Yeah?" I asked.

He glared at me. "Marissa fucked shit up. Not you. You tried to do right by her. She's the one that dragged you through the mud. Don't ever get that shit twisted, got it?"

I nodded. "Got it."

He patted my cheek. "Good. Now, say it out loud. I want to hear you admit it."

I cracked my neck. "All right, here goes. You ready?"

He smiled. "Hit me with it."

I drew in a deep breath. "I've fallen in love with Eva."

His jaw hit the floor. "Uh, say what now?"

I paused. "What?"

"Did you just say you loved the woman?"

I cocked my head. "What the hell did you think I was going to say?"

"That you wanted to sleep with her!"

I waved my hand in the air. "Oh, that ship has already sailed."

He balked. "Oh, you've been fucking holding out on me, man. I'm hurt, Gavin. Genuinely hurt."

"Do you talk about you and your woman's sex life to me?"

"Oh, hell no. That shit's sacred."

"Well, that's how I feel about Eva."

He licked his lips. "Shit, you really do love her, don't you?"

I set my empty can on the coffee table. "Yeah, I do. But I don't know what to do about it. I don't want another Marissa situation on my hands. I don't want another broken heart, and I certainly don't want another woman that Asia already loves as well to up and leave because of bullshit I pull. I didn't think this through, Jorge. I figured we'd fuck around a bit, get it out of our systems, and go on with our lives."

"But, that's not what happened?"

I shook my head. "Not in the slightest. It grew into something that I almost can't manage, and I don't want to do anything to jeopardize the little bit of stability I have managed to get into Asia's life in the first place. I can't bear the idea of rocking her world again, and for the worst."

Jorge leaned back and sighed. "All right, I see why you wanted to talk."

I folded my arms across my chest. "I've got this job and my feelings for Eva. I know this job is going to take me away for a few months. Asia will be in school, and she'll be here without me. What if Marissa tries to swoop in and do shit while I'm gone? Will I even be able to get Eva the power of attorney she needs to deal with my ex's bullshit?"

"Whoa, whoa, whoa. Slow down. You're going a bit too quickly. Let's take this one step at a time. Okay? Have you thought about just taking Eva and Asia with you while you film? I'm sure Eva could homeschool your daughter while you're working."

I shrugged. "I mean, I thought about asking her, but I'm not sure how it would go over. Plus, she'd have to get certified to homeschool Asia. That certification would have to happen in California. I think you have to be a resident, and I'm just not sure if that's feasible in this kind of time span."

"All right, but you also won't know shit until you involve Eva in this conversation and just ask. Does she know about this job?"

"I haven't told her or Asia yet, no."

He snickered. "Then, I'd start there and see what happens. You're torturing yourself over what if's when you've got someone who can answer those questions living under your damn roof now. See what I'm saying?"

I checked my watch. "If she'd ever get home from this doctor's appointment."

He paused. "How long has she been gone now?"

"Almost three hours."

"That's a pretty long appointment."

I sighed. "I know, but I also gave her the day off to unpack and get settled in. Maybe she's just running errands."

"You sure about that?"

My eyes locked with his. "What does that mean?"

Jorge leaned forward. "For a guy who needs all the pieces in play before he makes a move, you're doing a lot of assuming lately. If you're worried about her, just call and make sure she's okay. I'm sure she'll appreciate the concern."

Then, I spat out the big thing hovering around in my mind. "But, why go through all of this in the first place if I'm just going to up and move to California and leave all of this behind?"

Silence fell between us for a while before Jorge cleared his throat. He stood to his feet and backtracked into the kitchen to get us another set of beers, and even after he cracked his open, he didn't speak.

It wasn't until after he took a long pull from his can that he spoke. "I actually think that's a good idea."

I narrowed my eyes. "Wait, you do?"

He shrugged. "I mean, it makes sense. The bulk of your work is there, and Key Biscayne is a bit far away from your work."

I chuckled. "And a fresh start after I get full custody of Asia would be nice."

"I hear a 'but' coming."

"But, I also don't want to leave Eva behind. I'm serious when I say I love her. I want her to be included in this shit."

He patted my knee. "Then, it sounds like you need to be talking to Eva instead of me about all of this."

"And I'm not gonna lie, I feel like shit for ditching her for two weeks after everything that's gone on between us. Then, doing it again at the end of the year? Through the holidays? That just doesn't seem right."

"Which means we're back to you taking them with you, dude. Just do it. As long as Asia is taken care of, protected, and being schooled in some way, what's the problem? You're making this into a much bigger thing than it needs to be, I'm telling you."

I set my unopened beer between my legs. "I don't know. I don't know how to explain it, but something just doesn't feel right in all of this. And you know me, I can't make a move until it all feels the way it's supposed to feel. I mean, I just got the girl moved into a bedroom upstairs, and now I'm uprooting her to Hollywood? That doesn't seem fair at all."

"I suppose that depends on how you want to treat her."

"What?"

He smirked. "Do you want to treat her like a girlfriend or an employee? Because an employee would step to the beat of your drum without hesitation, but a girlfriend is who you talk shit over like this with. Is she your employee, or is she your girlfriend?"

I scoffed. "Is it bad that I can't even answer that question without it being complicated?"

He barked with laughter. "If you want to know what I think, here it is. I'm not the person you need to be talking to. This word vomit is meant to help you both clarify your thoughts and feelings. And if you really want to include her in all aspects of your life, then you need to talk with her the second she gets home. Don't let another day go by without her knowing what the hell's going on around her. She won't appreciate it being dropped into her lap at the last minute because you couldn't man up and talk to her."

I felt more confused than ever before, but Jorge also had a good point. He could be a shoulder for me to lean on, but all of my answers would come when I spoke with Eva. I checked my watch, and worry started pooling in my gut. I pulled out my cell phone and checked my text messages, wondering if maybe I wasn't feeling it vibrate or some shit.

And just as I went to dial Eva's number, a call came through my phone from a number I didn't recognize. "Well, that never happens," I murmured.

"What?" Jorge asked.

I turned the phone to face him. "A number I don't know."

He furrowed his brow. "Give me that. I'll answer it for you."

I passed the phone off to him even though a sinking feeling filled my stomach.

"Hello?" Jorge asked when he answered.

I sat on the edge of my seat, watching his reactions. He stood to his feet slowly before he snapped his fingers, beckoning me to get up. And when I shot to my feet, he started nodding.

"Uh-huh. Uh-huh. I see. Yeah, I got it. Uh-huh, he's right here."

"Who is it?" I mouthed.

He put his finger up at me. "Uh-huh. Yep. I'll tell him now. Yes, he's on his way. Then—thank you. We appreciate it."

Then, he hung up the phone call and tossed me my phone. "Well?" I asked.

He chewed on the inside of his lip. "I'll stay here with Asia, but you need to get to the hospital."

I felt the world bottom out below me. "I'm sorry, what?"

He gripped my shoulders and shook me a bit. "Hospital, Gavin. Now. Eva's been admitted. She passed out at her doctor's appointment, and they called an ambulance. I've got Asia, but you need to go. Now."

And the next thing I knew, I bolted out the door and sprinted straight to the garage, trying to make it to Eva's side as quickly as I could get there.

## 22

**Eva**

My eyes opened slowly, and the first thing I smelled was disinfectant. The stench was so strong that it made my nose curl, and I shifted to get away from it. And when I moved, I heard a swarm of footsteps rocket toward me before a bright light shone in my eyes.

"Can you tell me your name?"

The deep, resonating voice rattled my ribcage. "Uh, Eva."

"Good, good. Can you tell me the last thing you remember?"

*The doctor's office.* "Sorry, where am I? Where's Dr. Lucy."

"At least she remembers that," a female voice said.

"Can you open your mouth?"

I did as the voice asked of me, but I felt panic rising in my gut. Where the hell was I? Who were these people? This didn't feel like Dr. Lucy's office. For one, the bed in there wasn't big enough to allow me to lay down. I shouldn't have been lying down in the office.

Then, I felt someone messing with the top of my hand.

"Stop," I murmured. And when I ripped it away, I brought my hand in front of my face only to see the IV protruding out of my skin. "I'm in a hospital?" I exclaimed.

"Where is she? Eva? Where are you?" Gavin's voice sounded so far away, and yet it was crystal clear.

I batted away the hands and the questions, frustrated that no one would answer mine. I tried to prop myself up, but a pair of hands pressed against my shoulders.

"You need to lie down. You've been out for quite some time."

"Eva!" Gavin exclaimed.

I cleared my throat. "Help! I'm in here, Gavin!"

The thundering of footsteps headed my way before people started grunting. I blinked to try to clear my vision, but it was fuzzy. Hazy. Like I had just taken a handful of narcotics or some shit like that. I put my hand up to try to take stock of the IV again, but instead, I felt something warm wrap around it. Something warm and familiar.

"I'm right here. It's okay. Everything's going to be just fine," he cooed.

"Mr. Lincoln," the booming voice said, "I didn't realize she was with you."

I looked over at Gavin. "What's going on? Why am I here?"

He furrowed his brow. "They haven't told you where you are yet?"

"She just woke up. We were trying to get a read on her vitals to make sure she didn't sustain any head trauma when she passed out," a female voice said.

Gavin didn't take his eyes off me. "Thank you, nurse. I'll take it from here, guys."

"We still have tests to run. We don't know why she fainted," the deep voice said.

I sniffled. "I do."

Gavin brushed my hair away from my forehead. "You know why you passed out in the doctor's office?"

I nodded slowly. "Can you get everyone to leave? We really need to talk."

With a flick of his wrist, the entire staff in my hospital room was gone. I heard a soft buzzing of the fluorescent lights blanketing us and rattling my eardrums. Gavin's eyes were filled with worry, but I knew soon they would be filled with anger.

*Is he going to leave me?*

*Fire me?*

*Make me get an abortion?*

*Tell me to fuck off?*

"It's okay; I promise you're safe. But, we're alone now. So, fill me in. What happened at your doctor's appointment?" he asked softly.

*How did I mess up so badly with those damn pills?* "No one should ever find out something like this in this fashion. I'm really, really sorry. Everything has been such a whirlwind that I didn't even realize it."

"Realize what, beautiful?"

"Please, don't hate me."

He snickered. "I could never hate you, Eva. Okay? Just—just put my mind at ease. Tell me what's going on."

My mind tried to formulate a plan as he kissed each knuckle on the hand of mine that he held. I had to find another excuse. I had to lie to him, just until I got out of this hospital. Then, we could have a formal conversation about it. Then, I could get myself out of the way if he decided he couldn't handle what was going on.

"What are these?" Gavin asked.

When I focused back on Gavin, I saw him picking up the bag. My eyes bulged as he reached inside, and it felt like the entire world had slowed down completely. I felt my heart screaming, no! I felt my gut screaming, "just do it!" The entire world I had created for myself was slipping between my fingers like sand on the beach.

And when he pulled out the bottles of prenatal pills at the bottom of the bag, his stare came back to mine. "Eva?" he asked.

I started rambling as tears lined my eyes. "I swear, I didn't plan this. After every encounter, I left to go get the Plan B pill. Well, I left to go back to my place, and then I went to get the Plan B pill because the pharmacies were never open that late. But, I did everything I could. I took that pill within twenty-four hours after every sexual encounter we had. I actually made the doctor's appointment to get on regular birth control pills! I was careful, Gavin. I promise you that I didn't plan this. It wasn't some trap. I'm not that woman; I'd stake my soul on it. And I can still work. I'll still take care of Asia, and nothing—not even any sort of morning sickness or whatever—will keep me from taking absolute care of your daughter. I just fainted when Dr. Lucy told me I was pregnant, that's all. That's literally all that happened."

By the time I was done rambling, I had started panting for air. I heard the beeping of my heart monitor slowly ticking up with each second that passed. I watched Gavin as he studied the bottle of pills in his hand. His eyes kept sliding from my face to the bag, back to my face, and then the bag again. As if he couldn't decide whether he was dreaming or awake.

"Please say something," I whimpered.

And when his stare came back to my watery gaze, he blinked. "You're pregnant?"

I nodded, trying to gain my composure. "Yes, I'm pregnant. But, I promise you I don't need to be fired. I might have to slow down a bit during my last trimester, but it won't get in the way of taking care of Asia. You don't have to do anything if you don't want to, either. I won't take your money, or take you to court, or do any of the things your ex has done to you. I just want to keep my job. That job is the only thing that will enable me to provide for this child if I actually carry it to term. I'm pretty sure I'm only, like, five weeks along. So, for all I know, I'll just have a late period, and that'll be that."

Gavin cocked his head. "We're—we're pregnant?"

A tear slid down my cheek. "Yeah. We're pregnant."

Then, the deep, resonant voice that greeted me the second I woke up filled the room again. "We'd like to get an ultrasound, too, just to make sure everything is okay."

I jumped at the sound of his voice. "Can you guys just leave us alone?"

Gavin rubbed his hand against my arm. "We just need a little longer, thank you."

The doctor nodded before backing out the door, and I closed my eyes. My head fell back against the pillows, and I couldn't contain my sobs any longer. The past few weeks had been such a whirlwind, and I had no idea my life could change so quickly, and all of the stressors just came pouring out in the form of tears.

"Please, don't cry," Gavin whispered.

He bent forward and kissed the shell of my ear, whispering sweet nothings as I turned toward him. I scooted to the edge of the hospital bed, wanting nothing more than his comfort as my life spiraled out of control. My sobs hiccuped my chest. My tears drenched the skin of my neck. I wailed out into the room, unable to contain the hurt and the confusion and the pain and the uncertainty of what was to come.

"Scoot over, let me get in with you," he whispered.

I didn't question his words, and I didn't question his motives. Instead, I did what I always did—I listened. I scooted over, and Gavin slipped beneath the covers with me before he cradled me in his arms. I placed my cheek against his chest and listened to the steady rhythm of his heart beating. The heart monitor in the background raged out of control as my pulse skyrocketed and plummeted with my panicked episodes. I cried until I couldn't breathe. I cried until I snorted and wheezed to try to get more air so I could cry harder.

And after my body finally settled down, Gavin kissed the top of my head. "We're really pregnant," Gavin whispered.

I sniffled and looked up into his face, readying myself to apologize again. But instead, I saw him staring at the ceiling with a smile on his face. With tears in his eyes. And it gave me hope.

"Yeah, we really are," I said softly.

He peeked down at me, and I giggled when I saw a tear streak his cheek. He smiled as he kissed my forehead again, and his smile filled me with hope. He wasn't angry with me. How was that even possible?

I reached up and brushed his tear away as he dried my cheeks with his own fingertips. I nestled tightly against him, feeling him pull me steadily closer. I took a chance and kissed the crook of his neck, seeking the smallest bit of his warmth for myself.

Then, his fingers gripped my chin before pulling my gaze upward. "We need to get you that ultrasound," he said.

And before I could speak, his lips fell against mine.

My heart stopped in my chest. My heart rate monitor

settled to almost nothing for a brief second, and I heard the door to my room slam open. That doctor outside started murmuring orders to his staff of nurses, asking them to get an ultrasound machine in the room and to fetch the OB on-call. I lost myself in the way Gavin's tongue massaged the roof of my mouth. I reveled in the way he sucked on my lower lip. I turned into him, ready to take him into my arms and make love to him right in that damn hospital bed until one of the nurses cleared her throat.

"I hate to interrupt, but we can make it quick," she said.

I giggled as Gavin nodded. "Of course. Let me get up. Will we be doing it in here?"

An unfamiliar face slipped into the room. "My name is Dr. Emilia Johnson. I'm the OB on-call this week. I'll only be doing this particular ultrasound, and then from here, the two of you can talk about who you might want to book regular appointments with. And I promise this hospital uses the utmost discretion. We take our confidentiality agreements very seriously."

Gavin stood up and held my hand. "I appreciate it, thank you."

I nodded. "Me, too. Thank you very much."

I watched as everyone got set up and readied all of the ultrasound equipment. The OB turned off the overhead lights, and the ultrasound technician asked for permission to roll up my shirt. The crystal-blue goop she squirted onto my stomach made me shiver from head to toe. But, the warmth of the ultrasound wand slowly warmed me up. Gavin held my hand, our fingers intertwined as the probe got pushed around and shoved into my abdomen as tightly as I could stand it.

Then, right there in the middle of the screen, it happened. A small black and white circle popped up.

"There's the little guy," the technician murmured.

She started taking multiple pictures and measuring things on the screen, but I was shellshocked. Holy shit, I really was pregnant. I looked down at my stomach before I looked back at the monitor and wondered when I'd feel activity on my own. It made me smile at the idea of having a little miniature Gavin bouncing around before too long.

"Wow," he murmured.

I looked up into his face.

He looked down at me with a great big smile on his face. "I bet he's just like his momma."

"Hey, what makes you think it's a boy?"

He grinned. "I just know these things. I knew Asia was a girl after only two months. Just call it 'father's intuition.'"

I giggled. "Pretty sure that's a Mom thing, too."

He shrugged. "Eh, it's a fifty-fifty shot either way. But it would be nice to have a boy and a girl running around. Don't you think?"

I swallowed hard. "Does that mean... we're really doing this?"

His brow ticked with confusion. "I'm honestly shocked anything else ever occurred to you."

"So—everything's okay?"

He nodded. "Uh-huh."

"And… I'm not losing my job?"

He smirked. "Nope."

"And… you're not kicking me out of the house?"

He bent forward, gazing into my eyes. "You're actually very stuck, so I hope you can deal with that."

I smiled so hard my eyes closed. "I can more than deal with that."

He captured my lips once more as the ultrasound technician wiped off my stomach. Gavin cupped the back of my head, supporting me as he deepened our kiss. My heart took flight as my shirt was pulled down. He slowly tilted me upright and turned me until my legs were dangling off the edge of the hospital bed.

And before I knew it, I was in a wheelchair with my discharge papers and everything I needed to get my pregnancy started, including our first-ever ultrasound pictures.

"You feel up to getting some food?" he asked.

Gavin wheeled me out of the hospital's back exit to avoid anyone with prying eyes and phone cameras.

"I could definitely eat. But what about Asia?"

Gavin chuckled. "Jorge's at the house with her. He'll stay there as long as we need him to stay."

A black Town Car pulled up as Gavin put the brakes on my wheelchair. A nurse helped me upright as an elderly man got out and jogged around to open my car door. I looked up at him to thank him, but my eyes caught his nametag.

And I smiled when I saw the name "Lucas."

"It's nice to finally put a face to the name," I said.

He nodded. "Likewise, Miss Eva."

I shook my head as I sat down on the leather seats. "Eva is just fine, Lucas."

Gavin quickly slipped in beside me. "Lucas? Take us somewhere you like to eat. We're all going out to celebrate for dinner."

With one last nod of his head, he closed the door and jogged back around to the driver's side. The doctors and nurses waved us off, and when Lucas pulled the car forward, I leaned my head on Gavin's shoulder. I closed my eyes and let my hand settle on my stomach. In a few months, my body would change and morph so much that I wouldn't even be able to wear the clothes I currently had on.

*We have so much to talk about.*

"How does Mexican sound?" Lucas asked.

Gavin kissed the top of my head. "That sit well with your stomach? I want you to eat something that won't make you sick so you don't pass out on us again."

I licked my lips. "I could go for a nice, big taco salad."

Gavin chuckled. "Mexican sounds great. Lucas, lead the way."

And I closed my eyes during the long, winding drive, allowing myself a moment to catch my breath and think of all the wonderful things to come—after Gavin and I got past the very awkward conversations that had to take place, first.

## 23

**Gavin**

"Is Lucas not eating with us?" Eva asked.

I took a bite of my chicken. "I told him we needed some private time, so he's eating in the car."

She pouted a bit. "Maybe we should go out and eat with him or something. I don't want him to be alone."

"He'll be okay. Right now, it needs to be just the two of us."

Eva gave me a hesitant look that told me just how nervous she still was, but I didn't know why. She didn't have to be. At least, not with me. I was ecstatic that we were pregnant, even though we hadn't known one another very long at all. Was it a shock to both of us? Of course. Was I worried about things?

Hell, yeah. Was I scared out of my mind to be attached to Eva for the rest of my life?

Absolutely not.

*Ask how she's feeling. Get the conversation going.*

But, when I spoke, she spoke as well, and the question that hit my ears made me gawk.

"How are you feeling?" I asked.

However, Eva blurted out... "You won't make me give it up or anything at the last minute, will you?"

I felt my jaw unhinge toward the floor. "Why in the world would you ever think I'd do such a thing?"

She put down her fork. "Can you blame me?"

"I don't know who I can blame, but I'd like to not blame anyone. Have I ever given you the impression that I'm that kind of person?"

She flopped back against her seat. "I don't know anything anymore. I don't know where we stand. I don't know where I stand in your life. I don't know where this will stand with Asia."

I held out my hand for her. "Come here."

Her eyes met mine. "Gavin, this changes so much."

I wiggled my fingertips. "Just come here, please."

She leaned forward and slid her hand against my own. "I can do this on my own if you aren't ready for another child. You don't have to be the hero of this story. I mean, I didn't see myself having children like this, or even this soon, but it happened, and I'm ready to take on the responsibility. I just don't want to ruin your life with something I thought I was combatting properly."

I scoffed. "Eva, you aren't doing this alone even if you wanted to. That child you're going to be growing is half of me, and no woman carrying my child is going to be doing anything alone. You got that?"

She swallowed hard. "So, we're really doing this? We're keeping the baby?"

I sighed. "I've always wanted more children. But, the life that I lead and my career path doesn't always make time for that kind of thing. It's hard just being there for Asia with the life I lead and how much I bounce around for my jobs and projects."

"So, we're fucked is what you're saying."

I snickered. "I'm not saying that at all. I'm just saying it's not going to be easy. Am I worried that it won't be fair to bring another child into the life I lead? Yeah, I'm worried. I see the toll it's taken on Asia over the years, but I also know a lot of that is because of her mother not protecting her the way she should have. Asia was a media pawn from a very young age, and it's made her very skittish and anxious about the outside world."

She shook her head. "I'd never do that to our child. Never. I'll protect both this little one and Asia like they're my own."

"Which is exactly why I hired you to be my nanny in the first place. You're good to my daughter. Better than her own damn mother is. And you're going to be a fantastic mother to our child. But, whatever else gets thrown our way, I'm ready for it. The question is, are you?"

Nervousness washed over her features as she pulled her hand away from mine again. She was afraid. She had more to lose in this scenario than I did. And for the life of me, I had no idea how to reassure her except be honest with her about my feelings.

"Would you like to talk about something else right now?" I asked.

She nodded mindlessly. "Yeah. I can't eat when I'm this worked up."

I took a sip of my Coke. "Very well. Then, I guess I should tell you that I heard back from my lawyer."

Her eyes lit up. "About the custody stuff? What did they say?"

"Well, Marissa sort of shot herself in the foot. She had her lawyer expedite the court hearing, so my lawyer was actually in court this morning. My lawyer presented all of the information as to why I should be awarded full custody as well as custodial parentship over Asia, and Marissa had such a meltdown in court that the judge ruled full custody to me until Marissa sought help for her—oh, what were the words he used—uh, 'obvious anger and control issues.'"

She snorted. "You're kidding. She went off in court like that on a judge?"

"My lawyer described it as more of a breakdown than anything else. And I knew it was coming. Marissa was never quite right after she gave birth to Asia, and I kept telling her to get help, but she just kept burying herself in other things. I think there are some unresolved anger issues, sure, but I also think there are some unresolved depression issues and things stemming from her childhood that she needs to get worked out as well."

"If she works them out, you think you'll ever go back to a shared-custody agreement?"

I thought hard about her question. "I'm not sure. I think visitation whenever Marissa's free to do so would be all I'd be able to offer. Asia needs a stable home. She doesn't need to be bouncing around between two families with two very different perceptions of life. It'll all be on a day-by-day basis, but for now, Marissa is forced to get the help she needs and Asia doesn't have to deal with her any longer. So, I'm happy."

Eva's smile was genuine, and it melted my heart even more. "Then, I'm happy as well. Have you broken the news to Asia?"

I shook my head. "Doesn't require a formal conversation in my eyes. She didn't ever like going with her mother, so one day, when she asks me why she hasn't seen Mom in a while, I'll just tell her that Mom's finally getting some help for some things and when she's feeling better, she'll be back around."

"You're a phenomenal father, Gavin. Never forget that, okay?"

My gaze hooked with hers. "So, with those words you just said, understand that I'm not abandoning you. You aren't fired. You aren't kicked out. None of the things you think might happen are actually going to happen. You've been part of this family from day one, and it's going to stay that way. All right?"

She sniffled. "You promise?"

I chuckled. "That, I can promise above everything else."

She stood from her chair and rounded around the table, so I pushed out my chair. She sat in my lap and placed her head on my shoulder before she started crying again, and the sound broke my heart. I wrapped her up tightly and pressed mindless kisses against her arm. I rocked her side to side as her tears wet my shirt, and I wished for nothing more than to take her sadness away.

"It's going to be okay," I whispered, "and I'm not going anywhere. I swear."

As I held the woman I loved in my arms, I thought about what it might be like to have a boy. I thought about all the things I wanted to teach him about being a man. About how to really romance a woman. About how to treat people with respect, which many men seemed to be lacking these days. But then, my mind turned to the idea of another little girl.

And I felt my protective instincts fill my gut.

The idea of having a house full of girls made me feel strong. Powerful. Protective, like a lion at the head of his pride. There weren't very many men in this world blessed with a family full of girls. If Eva were growing a sweet little girl inside of that body of hers, I knew I'd be the happiest man on the face of this planet. The idea that I could be so blessed to be seen as the kind of man that the cosmos deemed fit enough to protect a house full of women made me smile.

And as Eva's sobs started winding down, my hand gravitated toward her stomach, and my fingers splayed against her clothed skin.

"I'll protect both of you until the day I die," I whispered.

We didn't finish our food. In fact, I had our waiter pack things up in to-go boxes so we could take it with us. And after scooping Eva into my arms, I carried her back out to the car. I slid her into the backseat before I scooted in beside her, allowing her to lay her head in my lap as I played with her hair. The smell of Mexican food filled the space around us as Lucas silently drove us back to my place. We quickly interchanged with Jorge, who had been kind enough to watch Asia and put her to bed. I told him that I'd call later to fill him in, then I carried Eva upstairs to her new bedroom while Lucas put our leftovers in the fridge.

The knee-jerk part of me wanted to slip Eva into bed with me. But, I wasn't sure how she'd feel about that. I carried her into a room filled with nothing but boxes and almost used that as an excuse to take her back to my room. But, the bed was made up with pristine sheets, and everything else was ready to go. So, I settled her onto the mattress and tucked her in.

"So tired," Eva mumbled.

I kissed her splotchy forehead. "Get some rest. Don't worry about getting up with Asia. When you get up, we'll be downstairs."

She yawned. "No more coffee, okay?"

I chuckled. "Yes, no more coffee for you. I'll make sure there's some decaf made up."

She yawned again. "Night, night."

I kissed her one last time. "Night, night."

She snuggled down into the sheets, and I figured that was it. I thought she was dead asleep, and that meant she needed privacy. I took one last second to study her before I crept over toward the light switch, readying myself for a night alone to stew with my thoughts.

Then, I heard Eva mumble something in her sleep that stopped me in my tracks.

"Love you."

The hairs on the back of my neck stood on end. I froze in the doorway, watching her like a hawk. Waiting for her to turn over and smile at me or yell, "gotcha!" or any number of things that could have ruined this spectacular moment.

But, none of those things happened. All she did was slip into an effortless slumber with her shoulders rising and falling with her breathing.

"I love you, too, Eva," I whispered.

With a flick of my wrist, the light was off, and I blazed a trail toward my home office. I had a lot of phone calls to make and even more arrangements to toggle in the coming months. There was no way in hell I could jettison off and film some movie and leave Eva here with Asia. I mean, I'd miss the entire first and half of her second trimester! Not happening one single fucking bit. And as I slipped into my office chair, my hand reaching for my desk phone, I felt a sense of calm and peace wash over me.

This was the path I was destined for.

This was the path my life needed me to take.

And dammit, I sure as hell wasn't going to screw it up with some bullshit.

## 24

**Eva**

Something warm pressed against my cheek over and over, and it pulled me out of my slumber. The softest giggle on the face of this planet tickled my ears before the blankets around me started moving. And when I felt the small body press against my own, my heart warmed.

"Morning, Asia," I murmured.

She giggled. "Daddy made breakfast. Wanna know what he made?"

I peeked down at her with one eye. "I smell bacon."

She nodded. "Uh-huh."

I sniffed the air. "Mmm and eggs."

She smiled. "Uh, *huh*."

I sniffed a few more times. "And... fruit?"

"Bingo!"

Gavin's voice came wafting down the hallway. "Asia?"

She scrambled out of my bed. "Yeah, Daddy?"

"Are you bothering Eva like I told you not to?"

I giggled and cleared my throat. "She's never a bother, Gavin!"

Asia poked her head out the door. "Yeah, Daddy! I'm never a bother!"

His laughter echoed down the hallway. "Well, in that case, breakfast is ready if you two are hungry."

I threw the covers off my body. "Don't mind if I do."

My stomach growled ravenously at the lack of sustenance as Asia took my hand. With a massive smile on her face, she tugged me out of the bedroom, and we both stumbled down the hallway. Exhaustion hung over me like a canopy, following me wherever I went. But, I kept up with Asia as we rounded the corner, raced down the stairs, and found our way to the kitchen table where our plates were already up and piping hot.

"Yummy! This one's mine," Asia said.

She claimed the Disney princess plate filled to the brim with cheesy eggs before Gavin set down in front of a massive mound of meat and toast. However, when my eyes found my plate, I thought the portions were a bit small.

I also pointed to the mug with a string hanging out of it. "What's that?"

Gavin pointed with his knife. "That's jasmine tea sweetened with honey. I didn't have any decaf coffee, and the internet said it's only got about twenty-five or so milligrams of caffeine."

I eased myself into my chair. "Any excuse for why my plate is so much smaller than yours? Or even Asia's, for that matter?"

He chuckled. "Just want you to take it slow. The last thing we want is you inhaling food and then getting sick."

Asia nodded with her mouth full. "Yeah, Eva. Gotta be slow, okay?"

I grinned at her. "Are you gonna go slow with me?"

She slowed her chewing down, and it made my head fall back with laughter. I reached over and took her hand in mine before kissing her soft skin. Then my eyes gravitated to the small napkin sitting next to my tea. There were two massive, oval-looking pink pills sitting there, but it only took me a second to register what they were.

I picked up my prenatal vitamins and tossed them into my mouth before washing them down with the delightful jasmine tea. Then, I dug into the small plate of food in front of me. "Thank you for breakfast," I said.

Gavin nodded. "I hope it sits well. If it doesn't, let me know. Okay?"

I took a bite of my scrambled eggs. "Mmm, so good. There's cheese in these."

He grinned. "Always. Cheese makes everything better."

I picked up a slice of meat. "And bacon. Bacon elevates all things."

He pointed at me with his fork. "Now, you're getting the hang of it."

I took a bite of my bacon and winked at him, and for the first time since we kicked things off, I saw him blush. It was the most beautiful sight my eyes had ever beheld, and I vowed to one day make him blush like that again. Did he feel that way whenever he made me blush? Is that why he always tried?

The thought made me so warm inside that I thought I was going to melt into a puddle on the floor.

As I continued eating, I took stock of the world around me. The food. The tea. The vitamins left out for me. The care Gavin took in thinking through my portions. He was really doting on me, and I knew I could get used to this quickly. But, I was no longer afraid of getting used to it because I believed his words from yesterday. I believed him when he said we were in this together.

"I'm supposed to ask how you slept," Asia said.

Gavin chuckled. "You aren't supposed to phrase it like that."

I watched Asia shrug, and I giggled. "I slept very well. Thank you for asking. How did you sleep?"

She took a big bite of her eggs. "Good."

Gavin sighed. "Don't talk with your mouth full, princess."

"But, she asked me a question."

"Then, chew and swallow before you answer."

"Or, she just shouldn't ask questions while I'm eating."

I shrugged. "She does have a point there."

Gavin tossed me a playful glare. "I can't control you both. I can only do it one at a time. So, can we be on my side?"

I heard Asia swallow before she giggled. "Or, she can be on my side, and we can rule the *world*!"

I pointed at her. "I like her idea better."

Gavin rolled his eyes. "Women."

Asia mocked his eye movements. "Men."

I barked with laughter, and my shoulders shook as I leaned forward at the table. I'd never seen Asia so sassy before, and I couldn't contain myself. She was the cutest thing on the face of this planet, and it had me wondering if our child would be even half as cute as her.

"You want some more eggs? I kept them warm on the stove," Gavin said.

I looked down at my plate and took stock of my body. "Actually—and I can't believe I'm going to say this—but I'm kind of full. Is that normal?"

He winked at me. "I retained some of the knowledge I picked up the first go-around."

I blushed and hushed my voice. "Not in front of Asia."

But, she didn't seem to notice. "Eva, we're going to do so many fun things today."

I looked over at her. "Oh, really now? And what are we going to do today, Princess Eva?"

"Well, first we're going to color because that's just awesome. Then, we're going to paint Daddy a picture together of the two of us."

I nodded. "Nice, nice. Will there be snacks, though?"

She shook her head. "No snacks until ten, but then we can have some fruit. And then we'll play tag until lunch!"

"Wow, that's a lot of tag."

She nodded vigorously. "Uh-huh. Gotta burn off all those calories before we eat lunch. And for lunch, we're going to have pizza. Then, we're going to go to the museum and look at pictures. Then, we're going to come home and make more pictures so we can put them on the wall and make our own art gallery that Daddy can walk through tonight. After we eat dinner, of course. You always eat dinner before you go look at pictures."

I yawned. "Right you are on that one."

Listening to the little girl rattle off our plans for the day made me feel even more drained. But, I did my best to try to bury it. I swallowed my yawns and rubbed my eyes every time I felt them watering, trying to play off like I still hadn't quite woken up.

But, Gavin wasn't having it. "Hey, princess?"

"—and tomorrow evening, we're going t—yes, Daddy?"

He reached over and patted her arm. "Promise me that you'll go a little easy on Miss Eva for now, okay? She needs to get settled into her new room and new routine, after all. Remember how hard that is for you?"

Asia's voice grew sheepish. "Sorry, Eva."

I stood up and kissed her cheek. "No sorries necessary. Just give me a few days to get settled in, and I promise you, we'll have all of the fun in the world before you go back to school."

Her eyes lit up. "Really?"

I nodded. "Yes, really. But, for now, how does another movie marathon sound?"

She gasped. "With snacks?"

"With all the snacks."

"Yes, yes, yes, yes, yes! Daddy, I gotta go get changed! It's a pajama day!"

Gavin got up and helped her down off her little booster seat before she scurried off toward the stairs. I leaned back and closed my eyes, thankful that I had wrangled the excited ball of bouncing energy that was Asia Lincoln into having nothing but a restful day today. The sun was shining brightly outside, and part of me felt guilty for not getting her out into it.

But, I figured if she wanted to take a break and go out back, I could float around in the pool or something while she swam.

"So, I made some phone calls after you fell asleep last night," Gavin said.

I heard Asia rushing around upstairs before my eyes found his. "Oh?"

He nodded. "Yep. I made a lot of them, actually. And one of them was to the director of this film I've been cast in."

I felt my stomach lurch. "Oh."

He pulled his chair around until he sat next to me. "I called and told the director that I wouldn't be able to do the film in Hollywood because of my growing family."

Shock filled my system. "Wait, you what? Seriously?"

He placed his hand on my knee and squeezed. "Yeah, of course, I did. Eva, if I took that job, I'd be gone for your entire first trimester and part of your second one, too. I don't want to miss all of that. If people want me to film that badly, they can come here and film. But, I'm not traveling anywhere during this pregnancy. I missed a lot of it with Asia, and I don't want to miss anything with this one."

I placed my hand on top of his. "That makes me feel a lot better, thank you. How did they take it, though? What about your career?"

His smile settled into a grin. "Well, the good thing about being in demand is that sometimes people are willing to be more flexible than usual. So, after some talking and a lot of convincing, I got the director to agree that Miami is a far better place to shoot the upcoming movie instead of Hollywood Studios."

I gasped. "You didn't."

He chuckled. "Yep. I got them to change the film site. I mean, that'll be a lot of ferrying back and forth from the island to the mainland. But, now I can film, we can stay here, and everyone will have what they need. How does that sound?"

I leaned toward him and captured his lips in a searing kiss. "I think it sounds fantastic."

In one fell swoop, Gavin pulled me into his lap, and I melted against his strength. Our tongues melded together in a familiar tango they were growing accustomed to, and my heart took flight. I loved this man. I loved everything about him, perfect and imperfect. And the idea that he would have turned down a movie just to stay by my side helped cast aside every worry I fell asleep with last night.

I whispered against his lips. "You're perfect; you know that?"

He kissed my forehead. "I'm not perfect, but you are."

I giggled. "How about, we're perfect for each other? How's that sound?"

He nuzzled my eyes back up to meet his gaze. "I'll take it."

He brought me back in for another kiss, and I let it sweep me off my feet. I allowed myself to get lost in the taste of him. The feel of him. The strength of him, as I sat there in his lap. The faint singing of Asia upstairs as she put on a little show for herself backdropped his hand splaying against my stomach. He massaged my skin slowly, and I placed my hand on top of his so we could both cradle the newest addition to our patchwork family.

Then, Gavin kissed down my neck before he turned his attention to my little baby belly.

"Hello there. It's me. Daddy. I know we've only just met, but I can't wait to kiss your little cheeks. You're going to be so loved, and your big sister, Asia, is going to want to teach you about everything. I hope you're ready for lots of glitter, though. Because she's a big fan of it."

Tears rushed my eyes as he continued whispering his little conversation to my stomach. I inched myself back over into my chair, and he got down onto his knees, coming eye-level with my bellybutton. He rolled up my shirt and kissed my skin, sending shivers spiraling throughout my body.

And the more he spoke to our little unborn baby, the more I fell in love with him.

Watching him press kisses against my belly helped me to realize things would be okay. Hearing him talk about our little family, ready to welcome this child into the world, aided in cementing all of the things he had told me yesterday. No longer were they fantasy. No longer was the life I wanted to live out of reach for me. At last, I had finally found what I had been looking for all this time—a man to love, a family to protect, and a future to look forward to.

*Everything is going to be okay.*

And even though I didn't know how we'd tell Asia, or how we'd break it to family, or even how we'd tell the public, I knew one thing was for certain—no matter what came our way, Gavin would walk us through it.

EPILOGUE

**Gavin**
**One Year Later**

"And cut! Good job today, everybody! Go home and be with your families!"

I stood and clapped my hands before I slid out of my director's chair. Everyone whooped and hollered as we finished up the last day of filming on my studio's first-ever project. The main cast came by and high-fived me and patted me on the back. The stagehands gave me thumbs-ups and smiles as I passed them, thanking them for the hard work they had put into this movie set.

And as everyone wished one another a beautiful holiday season, I heard my daughter yelling for me in the distance.

"Daddy! Are you coming home now?"

I whipped around and saw Asia rushing for me with a massive smile on her face. And in tow were the two other leading ladies in my life. Eva, who had grown into her post-baby curves in ways that made me salivate at night, and Asana, our bouncing, beautiful infant baby girl.

"Oh, come here, you big girl," I groaned as I hoisted Asia against me.

She hugged my neck tightly and peppered kisses along my cheek as Eva smiled at me. She lit up a room every time she walked into it, but seeing her cradling our precious little Asana made my heart fill with delight.

"Hey there, handsome. Heard you were wrapping up something big today. Thought we'd come to surprise you," Eva said.

I kissed her delicate lips before Asia wiggled her way down. "And who is this beautiful little thing? Hi there, baby girl. How are you? Did you sleep for Mommy this morning?"

Eva passed me our three-month-old daughter, and I felt myself falling in love all over again. She had a mound of blond hair on top of her head like my own, but she got her crisp green eyes from her mother. She came out with them, and I knew she'd be stuck with them, and the way my daughter smiled up at me while in my arms made my heart melt all over again.

"I love you so much," I whispered.

I kissed her chubby little cheek before I handed her back

to Eva, then I scooped Asia into my arms once more. She was much too big to be carrying around, but so long as my daughter wanted to be held, I'd be pumping iron in the gym and gaining muscles in order to make it happen. She laid her head on my shoulder and sighed, and the heat of her breath reminded me of all the glorious things that had happened over the past year.

Eva had given birth to a healthy baby girl.

Asia had settled into school, as well as her big sister role.

And me, opening up my own filming studio in Miami.

Everything seemed perfect in our lives, except for one thing.

"So," Eva said as she cleared her throat, "for the fourth time today, Jorge has called me to figure out what in the world our Thanksgiving plans are. And I hope you have an answer for him because I'm about to block his number. She said it with the coolest smile against her cheeks, and I almost barked with laughter.

"I'll talk with him once we get home, I promise."

She sighed. "Great, because I'm about to toss him off a cliff."

Asia giggled. "She's mad at Jorge. He called at six this morning."

I blinked. "Wait. Did he really?"

She smiled, but her eyes grew wide with muted fury. "An hour before our beautiful little girls woke up, yep."

I pulled my phone out of my back pocket. "I'll resolve it right now."

She kept that plastered smile on her face. "Much appreciated, and—Asia! You can't play on the set!"

Eva piled Asana into my free arm and went chasing after Asia as I dialed Jorge's number. The last thing I needed was him pissing off the woman I wanted to spend the rest of my life with because he was getting more anxious than I was. I peered over my shoulder and saw Eva racing after Asia behind the set scenes, so I maneuvered myself into a darkened corner where no one would see me before Jorge picked up.

"Dude, please tell me she's gone from the house."

I nodded. "Yeah, she's gone. But did you really call at six in the morning?"

"I didn't have a choice! You weren't picking up, and you said she was supposed to go to work with you all day today."

I looked behind me to make sure Eva hadn't resurfaced. "I know, I know. Plans changed, I'm sorry. But she's at the studio now, and I'm going to do my best to keep her with me for the rest of the day. Do you still have time to get it done?"

He shuffled around on his end. "We're headed there now. We need at least a couple of hours, though. Possibly three."

"Don't worry. Eva never turns down food, and a lot of the restaurants around where we are will take at least three hours to get in and get out."

"Wonderful. See you around five, then?"

I looked at my watch. "Make it six-thirty."

"Even better. See you soon."

"Jorge?"

He paused. "I know. And you don't have to say anything."

I sighed with relief. "I appreciate that."

"All right. Talk soon."

I nodded. "Talk soon."

And the second I hung up the phone, Eva's panting voice resonated behind me. "Did you talk to him about waking me up before seven again?"

I turned around with a chuckle on my lips. "I gave him a stern talking to, I promise."

She giggled. "My hero."

I leaned in and kissed her forehead. "My queen."

"Gavin! We need you over here!"

My head went on a swivel as I mindlessly handed Asana back to Eva. "What?"

Then, I saw a pair of hands waving in the air. "Over here! We need some input!"

Eva smiled. "Duty calls."

I tucked a strand of hair behind her ear. "I'll be right back. Stay here, and don't leave without me. I want to take my family out for some food."

"But, the restaurants will all be jam-packed right now."

I backed away and pointed at her. "Food time! No buts about it!"

"Well, then hurry up, so we don't have to wait for an hour!" she exclaimed.

I jogged over to where my assistant director was, and I watched a few clips with her while she rattled off a few things that needed to be changed. But, my eyes kept gravitating back to Eva. There she was, cradling our perfect daughter while wrangling Asia, with her hair tied up in a messy bun and her clothes hanging off her body. She was the epitome of beauty to me, and the ring box in my pocket for tonight seemed to almost vibrate against my thigh.

"—and this is where we need to re—Gavin? Gavin, are you even listening?"

I cleared my throat and shook my head. "Uh, yeah. You were, uh, talking about changing the lighting on this particular scene. But, I don't agree with that analysis. The lighting is darker in this scene because the reveal has to be nice and bright."

She nodded slowly. "Right. Except, that's not the scene we're watching right now."

I blinked. "Oh."

She snickered. "Something on your mind a bit?"

My gaze moved back to Eva. "A bit, yeah."

She placed her hand on my shoulder. "Want my advice?"

I looked back over at her. "Sure. Hit me with it."

Her hand slid back to her side. "Whatever you're thinking about, it can't wait. If there's anything this movie taught us, it's that life is way too short to try to plan things to be perfect. Whatever it is, just do it."

And she was right.

"Gavin, where are you going? We aren't done talk—Gavin!"

I held my finger up in the air. "I'll be right back, but this can't wait any longer."

I jogged back up to Eva, and she greeted me with that

breathtaking smile she always had for me whenever I reappeared out of thin air. She leaned in like always to kiss my lips, but I cupped her cheeks and pressed my tongue between her lips. Her hand slid up my abs and up my chest until she gripped my shirt and pulled me closer.

Then, I slid my hand into my pocket and pulled out the ring box.

"Mmm, what was that for?" she hummed.

But, I simply got down onto one knee and held up the little box.

"Gavin?" she asked.

Asia squealed. "Daddy! You're doing it!"

And the entirety of the studio paused in shock as I cracked open the black velvet box.

"Oh, my God. Gavin," Eva said breathlessly.

I smiled with tears in my eyes. "Jorge is going to be so pissed off with me for this, but I can't wait for a second longer."

She cupped her hand over her mouth. "Why would he be upset?"

I chuckled as a tear streaked my cheek. "Because he's currently decorating the house with Ginger and Margo in order to prepare for this moment right here. But, this moment can't wait for a second longer. I can't wait for a second longer, Eva."

Her hand fell from her face, and I saw her lower lip quivering. "Go on. Please."

I sniffled and took her hand. "Eva, you've been wonderfully supportive of me this past year. Dealing with my insecurities and the whirlwind that was Marissa with that custody agreement, and even my selfish whim to open up a filming studio right here where we live. You've fought for me, battled with my family for me, and all while I was off chasing my dreams even when I didn't know what my dreams were. You gave me a healthy daughter, you've brought joy into Asia's life, you've brought light back into mine. And had it not been for you, I'm pretty sure I wouldn't have my own studio."

I stood to my feet and plucked the ring out of the box before I hovered it just beyond her left-hand ring finger. "Eva Johnson?"

She giggled through her tears. "Yes."

"Will you marry me?"

And when her eyes met mine, she snickered. "I already said 'yes.'"

I blinked. "Wait, that 'yes' wasn't a question?"

She shook her head. "There's never been a question in my mind about you. And there never will be. Yes, Gavin, of course, I'll marry you."

The second I slid that beautiful pink diamond onto her finger, the entire studio erupted into applause. I scooped her into my arms, trying my best not to completely crush Asana as my lips fell against hers. Our tongues danced a familiar tango they had memorized over the past year. As Asia cheered and whistled for the two of us, flashes of our life together bombarded my memories.

Holding her hand and cheering her on while she pushed

Asana out of her body.

Holding her at night while she cried because she and Asia had gotten into their first fight.

Seeing her haphazardly throwing breakfast together in the mornings with her wild hair sticking out in all sorts of directions.

Making sweet, passionate love to her in the shower every time I felt like slipping in behind her.

But then, the scenes changed. As I held Eva in my arms and our lips pressed closer together, the cheering and the clapping and the whistling faded into the background. Eva's soft moans trickling down the back of my throat shook me to my core as she cupped my cheek, allowing me to feel the rose gold band of her ring against my skin.

And my mind opened itself up to a future I never once dreamt for myself until Eva came into my life.

I saw Asana walking for the first time. I saw Asia on her first day of high school. I saw Eva complaining about her first set of gray hairs and how she wanted to get them dyed to keep up her youth. I saw Asia playing softball and the two of us cheering from the stands. I saw Asana doing gymnastics and dancing while we all waved flags in the stands at her competitions.

I saw Eva's wrinkling hand in my own as new liver spots appeared every single day. I watched her hair completely gray out as her cheeks downturned, and her skin grew pale with age. I saw awards of every single kind spanning across multiple walls of our home. Awards from school for the girls, awards from Eva's community service for all the good she brought to our little slice of heaven, and awards from all across the globe on my directorship in my filming studio.

I saw us surrounded by all of us while we laid in bed with one another, staring into each other's seventy-year-old eyes and still kissing as if we had just met.

I saw it all in my mind as I kissed her. I tasted all of it as the band of her ring caressed my skin. And when she pulled back to brush her tears of happiness away from her skin, the dull roar of the studio came rushing back.

"I love you so much," Eva choked out.

I kissed her cheek before I bent down and kissed Asana's. "I love you, too. I love you guys so much."

Asia wrapped herself around my leg. "Daddy?"

I placed my hand on top of her head. "Yes, princess?"

She leaned her cheek against my side. "Can we go home now?"

I chuckled. "Yes, we can."

"To the Lincolns!" my assistant director exclaimed.

"To the Lincolns!" everyone else yelled.

Eva giggled. "You really have a peppy bunch here, don't you?"

I picked Asia back up into my arms. "And I wouldn't have it any other way."

"Here," my assistant director said as she walked up, "at least enjoy a drink with us before you two head out."

"What is it?" Eva asked.

I sniffed it. "Is this the leftover white-grape-and-mango juice from lunch?"

She nodded. "That, it is. Isn't this stuff insanely good? I can't get enough of it."

"Can I try?" Asia asked.

I held it up to her lips for her to sip. "You can have all of it if you'd like. I had four cups of it at lunch."

And Asia answered me by taking the cup from my hands and chugging it until it was gone.

"Wow, this is good. Where did you guys get this?" Eva asked.

Asia smacked her lips together before licking them. "That's fresh, isn't it?"

I winked at my daughter. "Good job, kiddo. You know your fresh fruits. Yep, it was freshly pressed just for lunch. It's a great combination, too."

Eva looked inside her glass. "I'll have to make that at the house. What's the ratio of grapes to mangos?"

My assistant director held out her hand. "The catering company is still here. I'm sure someone on their staff would be delighted to indulge you in that. Come, come."

Eva passed off Asana to me, and I watched the two of them walk off. Mandy, my assistant director, and Eva, my fiancé. I smiled at the idea. I had purchased that ring just before she gave birth to our daughter, and it had been sitting in my pocket every single day since. I didn't want to chance her cleaning the house or rummaging around for something and coming across it, so I kept it on my person whenever I left the house. And the damned thing had been taunting me and mocking me for a solid three months.

But, it was all worth it to see Eva peer over her shoulder and smile at me before wiggling her ring around for the lights of my studio to reflect off of it.

"I knew she'd love it," I murmured.

I watched them walk away as I cradled my two daughters. One at my side, and the other in my arms. I stood there like a man on a mission, waiting for one of my most important women to come rounding back around that corner. I would always be protective of my family. I would always be protective of what we had created and what we deemed as ours. And as Eva came walking back over to us, she pecked me on the lips before taking Asana out of my grasp.

"So, I have just one question for you," she said.

I tucked a strand of loose hair behind her ear. "Name it."

She peeked up at me. "Now that I have that delectable recipe that's totally going to be something we serve at our wedding, I need to know something."

I chuckled. "And what's that?"

She smiled brightly. "Can we do a fall wedding on the beach? I've kind of always wanted to do one of those."

The idea seemed so simple and so perfect that I could only think to capture her lips once more in a kiss. So, that's exactly what I did before cupping her cheek.

"Anything you want, my future wife. You can have anything you want for this wedding."

"Will I get to be in the wedding, pleaseeee?" Asia asked.

And as the two of us laughed with one another, I listened to Eva assure Asia she would be in the wedding. Then she rattled off all sorts of wedding plans while I escorted our little family out to my car so we could go forth and forage for food.

The family that I loved.

The family that I protected.

The family that I treasured.

"So, exactly how upset is Jorge going to be?" Eva asked.

I opened the door for her as I contemplated her question. "On a scale of one to ten? Possibly a six."

She started putting Asana in her car seat. "Any way to make that at least an eight? He needs to pay for waking me up this morning."

I grinned. "Well, he absolutely hates pranks. And he definitely wouldn't want anyone messing with his new garden that is finally sprouting this year."

She peeked up at me. "Want to go buy fake spider webs and put them all over his tomatoes."

I chuckled and kissed her forehead. "You, my dear, are perfection."

She patted my chest with her hand. "Let's swing through somewhere, get something quick, then go shopping for spider webs. I'm sure plenty of the holiday stores still have them in stock."

"They always say, 'those who prank together, stay together.'"

Eva giggled. "Then, I guess you're stuck with me."

Then, I gripped her chin and gazed into her eyes as I meant every syllable of the words that dripped from the tip of my tongue. "And I wouldn't have it any other way, Eva."

My life was perfect.

And I needed nothing else except for this.

Made in the USA
Las Vegas, NV
08 July 2021